DRAGONS
& DREAMS

DRAGONS

A COLLECTION OF NEW FANTASY

1 8 🚩 1 7

HARPER & ROW, PUBLISHERS

Cambridge, Philadelphia, San Francisco, London, Mexico City, São Paolo, Singapore, Sydney

NEW YORK

& DREAMS

AND SCIENCE FICTION STORIES

edited by

Jane Yolen,
Martin H. Greenberg
and Charles G. Waugh

Acknowledgment

"Laughter in the Leaves" by Charles de Lint first appeared as a limited edition chapbook from Triskell Press. Copyright © 1984 by Charles de Lint. Reprinted by permission of the author.

DRAGONS AND DREAMS
A Collection of New Fantasy and Science Fiction Stories
Copyright © 1986 by Jane Yolen, Martin H. Greenberg, and Charles G. Waugh
"The Box" © 1986 by Bruce Coville
"The Thing That Goes Burp in the Night" © 1986 by Sharon Webb
"Baba Yaga and the Sorcerer's Son" © 1986 by Patricia A. McKillip
"All the Names of Baby Hag"© 1986 by Patricia MacLachlan
"The Three Men" © 1986 by Zilpha Keatley Snyder
"Great-Grandfather Dragon's Tale" © 1986 by by Jane Yolen
"Carol Oneir's Hundredth Dream" © 1986 by Diana Wynne Jones
"The Singing Float" © 1986 by Monica Hughes
"Uptown Local" © 1986 by Diane Duane
Designed by Joyce Hopkins
1 2 3 4 5 6 7 8 9 10
FIRST EDITION

Library of Congress Cataloging in Publication Data
Main entry under title:
Dragons and dreams.

   Summary: A collection of ten science fiction and fantasy stories by authors such as Patricia A. McKillip, Jane Yolen, and Diane Wynne Jones.
   1. Science fiction, American.   2. Science fiction, English.   [1. Science fiction.   2. Fantasy.   3. Short stories]   I. Yolen, Jane.   II. Greenberg, Martin Harry. III. Waugh, Charles.
PZ5.S7   1986   [Fic]   85-45384
ISBN 0-06-026792-5
ISBN 0-06-026793-3 (lib. bdg.)

For Homer,
    Aesop,
    Mme. LePrince de Beaumont,
    Hans Christian Andersen,
    Washington Irving,
    Jules Verne, and
    H. G. Wells—

    all prize wonderers as children.

Contents

Introduction

What do dragons and dreams have in common, besides beginning with the letter D? They stir in us a sense of wonder.

Albert Einstein once wrote that "imagination is more important than knowledge," yet it is his work that has helped us dream realistically about going to the stars.

Think of it: If children from the fifteenth century could be magically transported into our time, they would be positive that they had come upon a world filled with magic. They would find moving pictures on impenetrable screens, words spoken from afar carried across tiny wires, enormous metal birds that carry people undigested in their silver bellies, and small fires contained in boxes. We see such things every day—televisions, telephones, airplanes, and cigarette lighters.

Not sorcery at all, but science. We live comfortably with our everyday magic.

Who knows what marvels, what mysteries, and what powers might be harnessed in the centuries ahead? No one alive knows—but we can all imagine.

So here are ten stories of marvels past, present, and future, nine written expressly for this volume and a tenth that arrived on one of the editors' doorstep as a Christmas present and positively shouted to be included in the book. What they have in common is the thread of wonder that weaves in and out of their tapestries. Take that thread, and, like Theseus in the old tale of the maze, let the thread lead you through tunnels filled with colorful imaginings and out again into the light.

Jane Yolen
Martin H. Greenberg
Charles G. Waugh

DRAGONS
& DREAMS

1
The Box

by Bruce Coville

Once there was a boy who had a box.

The boy's name was Michael, and the box was very special because it had been given to him by an angel.

Michael knew it had been an angel because of the huge white wings he wore. So he took very good care of the box, because the angel had asked him to.

And he never, ever opened it.

When Michael's mother asked him where he had gotten the box, he said, "An angel gave it to me."

"That's nice, dear," she answered, and went back to stirring her cake mix.

Michael carried the box with him wherever he went. He took it to school. He took it out to play. He set it by his place at mealtimes.

After all, he never knew when the angel would come back and ask for it.

The box was very beautiful. It was made of dark wood and carved with strange designs. The carvings were smooth and polished, and they seemed to glow whenever they caught the light. A pair of tiny golden hinges, and a miniature golden latch that Michael never touched, held the cover tight to the body of the box.

Michael loved the way it felt against his fingers.

Sometimes Michael's friends would tease him about the box.

"Hey, Michael," they would say. "How come you never come out to play without that box?"

"Because I am taking care of it for an angel," he would answer. And because this was true, the boys would leave him alone.

At night, before he went to bed, he would rub the box with a soft cloth to make it smooth and glossy.

Sometimes when he did this he could hear something moving inside the box.

He wondered how it was that something could stay alive in the box without any food or water.

But he did not open the box. The angel had asked him not to.

One night when he was lying in his bed, Michael heard a voice.

"Give me the box," it said.

Michael sat up.

"Who are you?" he asked.

"I am the angel," said the voice. "I have come for my box."

"You are not my angel," shouted Michael. He was beginning to grow frightened.

"Your angel has sent me. Give me the box."

"No. I can only give it to my angel."

"Give me the box!"

"No!" cried Michael.

There was a roar, and a rumble of thunder. A cold wind came shrieking through his bedroom.

"I must have that box!" sobbed the voice, as though its heart was breaking.

"No! No!" cried Michael, and he clutched the box tightly to his chest.

But the voice was gone.

Soon Michael's mother came in to comfort him, telling him he must have had a bad dream. After a time he stopped crying and went back to sleep.

But he knew the voice had been no dream.

After that night Michael was twice as careful with the box as he had been before. He grew to love it deeply. It reminded him of his angel.

As Michael grew older the box became more of a problem for him.

His teachers began to object to him keeping it constantly at his side or on his desk. One particularly thick and unbending teacher even sent him to the principal. But when Michael told the principal he was taking care of the box for an angel, the principal told Mrs. Jenkins to leave him alone.

When Michael entered junior high he found that the other boys no longer believed him when he told them why he carried the box. He understood that. They had never seen the angel, as he had. Most of the children were so used to the box by now that they ignored it anyway.

But some of the boys began to tease Michael about it.

One day two boys grabbed the box and began a game of keep-away with it, throwing it back and forth above Michael's head, until one of them dropped it.

It landed with an ugly smack against the concrete.

Michael raced to the box and picked it up. One of the fine corners was smashed flat, and a piece of one of the carvings had broken off.

"I hate you," he started to scream. But the words choked in his throat, and the hate died within him.

He picked up the box and carried it home. Then he cried for a little while.

The boys were very sorry for what they had done. But they never spoke to Michael after that, and secretly they hated him, because they had done something so mean to him, and he had not gotten mad.

For seven nights after the box was dropped Michael did not hear any noise inside it when he was cleaning it.

He was terrified.

What if everything was ruined? What could he tell the angel? He couldn't eat or sleep. He refused to go to school. He simply sat beside the box, loving it and caring for it.

On the eighth day he could hear the movements begin once more, louder and stronger than ever.

He sighed, and slept for eighteen hours.

When he entered high school Michael did not go out for sports, because he was not willing to leave the box alone. He certainly could not take it out onto a football field with him.

He began taking art classes instead. He wanted to learn to paint the face of his angel. He tried over and over again, but he could never get the pictures to come out the way he wanted them to.

Everyone else thought they were beautiful.

But they never satisfied Michael.

Whenever Michael went out with a girl she would ask him what he had in the box. When he told her he didn't know, she would not believe him. So then he would tell her the story of how the angel had given him the box. Then the girl would think he was fooling her. Sometimes a girl would try to open the box when he wasn't looking.

But Michael always knew, and whenever a girl did this, he would never ask her out again.

Finally Michael found a girl who believed him. When he told her that an angel had given him the box, and that he had to take care of it for him, she nodded her head as if this was the most sensible thing she had ever heard.

Michael showed her the pictures he had painted of his angel.

They fell in love, and after a time they were married.

Things were not so hard for Michael now, because he had someone who loved him to share his problems with.

But it was still not easy to care for the box. When he tried to get a job people would ask him why he carried it, and usually they would laugh at him. More than once he was fired from his work because his boss would get sick of seeing the box and not being able to find out what was in it.

Finally Michael found work as a night custodian. He carried the box in a little knapsack on his back, and did his job so well that no one ever questioned him.

One night Michael was driving to work. It was raining, and very slippery. A car turned in front of him. There was an accident, and both Michael and the box flew out of the car.

When Michael woke up he was in the hospital. The first thing he asked for was his box. But it was not there.

Michael jumped out of bed, and it took three nurses and two doctors to wrestle him back into it. They gave him a shot to make him sleep.

That night, when the hospital was quiet, Michael

snuck out of bed and got his clothes.

It was a long way to where he had had the accident, and he had to walk the whole distance. He searched for hours under the light of a bright, full moon, until finally he found the box. It was caked with mud, and another of the beautiful corners had been flattened in. But none of the carvings were broken, and when he held it to his ear, he could hear something moving inside.

When the nurse came in to check him in the morning, she found Michael sleeping peacefully, with a dirty box beside him on the bed. When she reached out to take it, his hand wrapped around the box and held it in a grip of steel. He did not even wake up.

Michael would have had a hard time paying the hospital bills. But one day a man came to their house and saw some of his paintings. He asked if he could buy one. Other people heard about them, and before long Michael was selling many paintings. He quit his night job, and began to make his living as an artist.

But he was never able to paint a picture of the angel that looked the way it should.

One night when Michael was almost thirty he heard the voice again.

"Give me the box!" it cried, in tones so strong and stern that Michael was afraid he would obey them.

But he closed his eyes, and in his mind he saw his

angel again, with his face so strong and his eyes so full of love, and he paid no attention to the voice at all.

The next morning Michael went to his easel and began to paint. It was the most beautiful picture he had ever made.

But still it did not satisfy him.

The voice came after Michael seven times that year, but he was never tempted to answer it again.

Michael and his wife had two children, and they loved them very much. The children were always curious about the box their father carried, and one day, when Michael was napping, the oldest child tried to open it.

Michael woke and saw what was happening. For the first time in his memory he lost his temper.

He raised his hand to strike his son.

But in the face of his child he suddenly saw the face of the angel he had met only once, so long ago, and the anger died within him.

After that day the children left the box alone.

Time went on. The children grew up and went to their own homes. Michael and his wife grew old. The box suffered another accident or two. It was battered now, and even the careful polishing Michael gave it every night did not hide the fact that the carvings were growing thin from the pressure of his hands against them so many hours a day.

Once, when they were very old, Michael's wife said to him, "Do you really think the angel will come back for his box?"

"Hush, my darling," said Michael, putting his finger against her lips.

And she never knew if Michael believed the angel would come back or not.

After a time she grew sick, and died, and Michael was left alone.

Everybody in his town knew who he was, and when he could not hear they called him "Crazy Michael," and whirled their fingers around their ears, and whispered that he had carried that box from the time he was eight years old.

Of course nobody really believed such a silly story.

But they all knew Michael was crazy.

Even so, in their hearts they wished they had a secret as enduring as the one that Crazy Michael carried.

One night, when Michael was almost ninety years old, the angel returned to him and asked for the box.

"Is it really you?" cried Michael. He struggled to his elbows to squint at the face above him. Then he could see that it was indeed the angel, who had not changed a bit in eighty years, while he had grown so old.

"At last," he said softly. "Where have you been all this time, Angel?"

"I have been working," said the angel. "And waiting." He knelt by Michael's bed. "Have you been faithful?"

"I have," whispered Michael.

"Give me the box, please."

Under the pillow, beside his head, the battered box lay waiting. Michael pulled it out and extended it to the angel.

"It is not as beautiful as when you first gave it to me," he said, lowering his head.

"That does not matter," said the angel.

He took the box from Michael's hands. Holding it carefully, he stared at it, as if he could see what was inside. Then he smiled.

"It is almost ready."

Michael smiled too. "What is it?" he asked. His face seemed to glow with happiness. "Tell me what it is at last."

"I cannot," whispered the angel sadly.

Michael's smile crumpled. "Then tell me this," he said after a moment. "Is it important?" His voice was desperate.

"It will change the world," replied the angel.

Michael leaned back against his pillow. "Then surely I will know what it is when this has come to pass," he said, smiling once again.

"No. You will not know," answered the angel.

"But if it is so important that it will change the world, then . . ."

"*You* have changed the world, Michael. How many people know that?"

The angel shimmered and began to disappear.

Michael stretched out his hand. "Wait!" he cried.

The angel reached down. He took Michael's withered hand and held it tightly in his own.

"You have done well," he whispered.

He kissed Michael softly on the forehead.

And then he was gone.

2
The Thing That Goes Burp in the Night

by Sharon Webb

He could hear it moving in the dark at the hollow of the stairs. He could hear it circling down there, snuffling, pausing, snuffling again. It was closer now. No more than a dozen steps away from his bed.

Shivering, John Thomas Caulfield clutched the thick quilt tighter and stared into the midnight room. He wanted it to go away. He wanted it to go away more than he had ever wanted anything in his whole life.

He never meant to call up the thing. Not really. He only did it to scare old Billy. Please, he thought. Make it go away. If it went away, he'd never ever be mean to his little brother again ever, no matter how rotten he was. "Oh, please," he whispered. "Make it go away."

Suddenly, a deathly quiet fell. John Thomas strained to hear. Then the sound came: a great intake of breath sucked through unspeakable nostrils. The thing was trying to get his scent. And when it did, it would know where to find him. . . .

It wasn't the Dutch-chocolate cake that made him do it. It wasn't even the sacred promise. It was because of the new baby. And why did his mom have to go and have an old girl, anyway?

John Thomas didn't have anything against girl babies. In general they were just as uninteresting as boy babies. He could take them or leave them, but what was hard to take was the way this one was messing up his life. It wasn't even in the house yet, and already things had changed.

It all started before supper. He had heard a thump in the kitchen and then a rattle-bang as the frying pan, whistle-clean from the cabinet, went sliding into the sink.

His mother stood there with her feet apart the way she'd had to stand since she'd got so big, and she was squeezing a package of pork chops. Squeezing hard. And her forehead was all squinched up.

"You okay, Mom?"

She caught her breath. Then she smiled. "I'm fine." But it was a funny smile, kind of lopsided and wobbly. The pork chops went plop onto the counter, and she spread her hands across her belly and cocked her head to one side as if she was listening to something.

He stood there, staring at her, not knowing what

to do, when she said, "Pizza. I think I'll have your daddy bring home pizza for supper. Okay?"

Before he could answer, she said, "Call your daddy and tell him for me. I'm going to go lie down for a few minutes." She headed out, but on the way she stopped and clutched at the doorjamb. "Call him, John Thomas. And tell him to hurry."

He grabbed for the phone and dialed the drugstore. The baby, he thought. It had to be. The baby was getting ready to come. The other pharmacist answered and it was a couple of minutes until he heard his father's voice.

"Mom said to bring home pizza. She said to hurry."

"Pizza?" There was a pause. "I'll be right there."

John Thomas's father dropped the pizza box onto the kitchen counter and hurried to the bedroom. In a minute or so he came out carrying a suitcase. "It's time for Mom to take a little trip." He grinned a nervous grin at his sons. "Before you know it, you're going to have a new brother or sister, boys."

Let it be a brother, thought John Thomas. Let it please be a brother.

His mom came into the kitchen then. The same funny little smile flitted across her face when she saw him. "Kiss good-bye?"

He gave her a kiss. Not sure of what to say then, he followed it with a quick hug.

"You too, Billy," she prompted. She turned to her husband. "Will they be all right, alone here?" Little worry lines traced across her forehead as she looked at her youngest. "Billy's not even seven yet."

"Sure we will," said John Thomas. The idea of a baby-sitter at his age was ridiculous. After all, he was nearly a teenager, wasn't he?

"They'll be fine," said his father. He lowered his voice. "You'll have to be the man of the house for a while, John Thomas. You can do it, can't you?"

He nodded. "Sure."

"No hitting Billy, okay?"

He nodded again. "Sacred promise, Dad."

"And Billy, you're going to be a good guy tonight. I know you are. For Mom's sake."

John Thomas stared as his mother gasped and a startled look passed over her face. "I think we'd better go now," she said to her husband. "Right away."

His father snatched up the suitcase again. "Lock the door behind us, boys. I'll give you a call as soon as I have news."

When his parents had gone, the house seemed especially empty. John Thomas lifted the lid of the pizza box. Pepperoni, his favorite. But somehow he didn't feel very hungry. When Billy popped open two Cokes though, and they started in on the pizza, his appetite came back with a bang.

He ate so much, in fact, that he didn't have any room left for dessert.

John Thomas stared at the big wedge of Dutch-chocolate cake. "I'll have mine later," he said. Knowing that Billy would hog the biggest piece, he eyed the cake carefully and sliced it precisely down the middle.

Balancing his cake and a king-sized glass of milk on a plate, Billy went into the living room and switched on the TV.

The movie, which was about a haunted house, started with the warning, "Parental Guidance Recommended. This film may not be suitable for young children."

"I guess that means you, squirt," said John Thomas. "Go do your homework or something."

A look of outrage came over Billy's face. "Who says?"

"I said. I'm the man of the house tonight, and what I say, goes. And don't talk with your mouth full."

"Yeah? Well, you're full of it. And—"

And just then, the phone rang.

Billy beat John Thomas to the telephone. "A what? We got a what?"

John Thomas snatched the phone away in time to hear "—sister. A beautiful baby sister."

He scarcely heard the rest of it, only bits and pieces about Mom being fine, about Daddy having to meet Grandma at the airport, about his not getting home until the middle of the night. All he could think about was the baby and how it was going to ruin his life.

Why did it have to be a girl, anyway? If it was a

boy, it would share a room with Billy. But an old girl got to have a room to herself. And that meant that he had to put up with Billy. Billy the Creep for a room-mate. Whoopee. It was enough to make him want to throw up.

He went back into the living room, ready to lay down the law about "parental guidance." But Billy wasn't there.

John Thomas settled back to watch the movie when a loud crash came from overhead. His room. His stuff! He tore up the stairs and threw open the door. "You creep."

His model robot lay on its side on the floor. The sheet metal was bent and the paint was scratched. He picked it up. The antenna was broken off at the base.

John Thomas raised furious eyes at Billy. "You stinking little creep. You broke it."

"I didn't mean to." Billy stared at the door and then back at John Thomas as if he was measuring the safety interval between them. "I was just moving it. It was on my side of the room."

"*Your* side?" yelled John Thomas. "I'm gonna kill you."

With a howl, Billy ran out of the room.

Fists doubled, John Thomas thundered down the stairs after him. It wasn't until he reached the bottom that he remembered his promise—his sacred promise to Dad. He stopped short then. "Curd face!" he hollered. He followed this with a string of four-letter words muttered under his breath so Billy wouldn't hear and tell.

Tonight he was the man of the house. And it stunk. But he was going to keep his promise if it killed him. He had promised not to get into a fight while Dad was gone. "You stinking slime!" he yelled. "Just you wait. Just you wait 'til tomorrow."

If Billy had been halfway decent after that, if he had been even a quarterway decent, then John Thomas would never have called up the monster.

John Thomas went back to his room. While he was trying to fix his robot, he heard Billy down in the living room. Let him watch the old movie, he thought grimly. He hoped it scared the pants off him. He hoped it scared him so bad he'd have nightmares. It would serve him right.

He pressed on the robot with both thumbs and the bent sheet metal gave a pop. It was still dented though. He'd have to fill it with putty and paint it all over again.

The putty was all the way down in the basement. As he went down the stairs, eerie music came from the TV, and a woman's voice said, "There's something strange going on in this house. I know it, Richard."

The kitchen light was on. And there stood Billy, stuffing his face with Dutch chocolate.

"That's *my* piece of cake!" yelled John Thomas.

"You didn't want it."

"What do you mean I didn't want it?"

Billy gobbled another bite.

As John Thomas's hands balled into fists, two things came to him: his promise to his father—and the strange, scary music from the TV. Suddenly a brilliant idea struck him, and he drew a deep breath. "Put down the cake, creep, before I do something that'll make you sorry you were ever born."

"Oh yeah?" Billy's bottom lip was studded with crumbs.

"Yeah." Then, whirling, John Thomas ran into the living room to the bookcase. He scanned the shelves frantically. He needed a book. One that looked right. There. His fingers paused at the thick, dark medical book that belonged to his father. He pulled it out and read the gold lettering on the cover: *The Merck Manual, Thirteenth Edition.*

Waving the book slowly from side to side in time to the weird movie music, he walked back into the kitchen.

The cake paused halfway to Billy's mouth. He eyed his brother and then the door. "What do you think *you're* doing?" His voice was belligerent, but he looked like he was ready to run at the first sign of violence.

"In here is the wisdom of the ancients." John Thomas rolled his eyes toward *The Merck Manual.* "The magic spells of alchemists and wizards. And I know how to use them."

Billy snorted. "Sure."

"I can call up anything I want, Freak Face. A monster—anything."

"You say."

"Just you wait." John Thomas flung open the top drawer of his mother's kitchen desk and began to rummage inside. In the back, behind a stack of Green Stamps books and a crumpled package of petunia seeds, he found a tall candle a little flattened on one side. "First, the magic black candle."

"It's not black," said Billy. "It's purple. And you better not mess around in Mom's desk or I'll tell."

"The magic black candle," John Thomas repeated ominously. Another foray into the drawer produced a bent package of matches. He tore one off and scraped it. The match flared and touched the wick. He switched off the kitchen light. The candle flamed and made dark, flickering hollows beneath his eyes.

"I think"—John Thomas's voice dropped to a menacing whisper—"I think I'll call up a special monster. Just for you. A monster with yellow fangs as long as that—" He waggled his outstretched hand, and long, curved finger shadows slid across the wall. "And you can't hide from it. Anywhere. You know why?" He narrowed his eyes. "Because its nose is big as your whole head. It's got a big, green, gummy nose. And it can smell the chocolate on your breath and find you. Even in the dark. And when it does, it's gonna eat your face."

"You're full of it," said Billy. But his voice quavered just a little bit.

"Yeah?" John Thomas thrust the candle into a jelly glass and thumbed open the book to the red-tabbed index marked "Rx." The thin paper crackled as he turned the pages deliberately. Then he stopped, fixed Billy with a long stare, and tapped a section with his index finger. "Here it is." Raising his eyes to the ceiling he said in a loud voice: "Monster-r-r. Hear me, Monster-r-r. Rise from the depths and get old Billy."

Billy's gaze slid uneasily toward the basement door.

"Cascara Sagrada"—John Thomas's voice deepened as he read—"Magaldrate. Oxethazaine in Alumina. Psyllium. Hydrophilic. Mucilloid."

A long wavering scream came from the TV.

Billy's eyes, wide now, glided back toward the flickering candle.

"Magnesia Magma," boomed John Thomas. "Kaolin."

Billy's teeth caught his lower lip.

"Pectin," John Thomas commanded. "Pectin . . . pectin . . . " he flung out his arms and bellowed, "Pectin-n-n-n. . . ."

A thick silence followed.

"It's coming now. It's gonna come when you're asleep. In the dark. . . ." John Thomas blew out the candle.

In the blackness that dropped like a thick curtain, he grinned at the little gasp that came from Billy's direction.

A scuffling sound.

The blue-white fluorescent light flashed on above the sink. Billy stood frozen, his hand on the light switch, his eyes staring wildly at the basement door. He blinked then, and looked down at the countertop and the wedge of Dutch chocolate. "I didn't want the old cake, anyway," he said, and slowly shoved the plate away.

"It's too late. There isn't any way to stop it now."

Billy's voice quavered. "Quit it, John Thomas."

"It's coming. It can smell the chocolate on your breath."

"Quit it. Quit." Then Billy was running out of the kitchen and up the stairs.

At the look on Billy's face, John Thomas felt a quick pang of guilt, but it passed in a moment and he reached for the uneaten cake. A minute later, he heard water running in the upstairs bathroom, and a little whishing sound.

Mouth full of Dutch chocolate, he grinned. Billy was brushing his teeth. Hard. As if his life depended on it.

Half wanting to watch the end of the ghost movie, half afraid to, John Thomas stared at the TV. He caught his breath as the music wailed into a wavering scream.

Then it was over. As the credits rolled, he got up and turned off the set. An eerie silence fell over the house.

Billy's probably asleep now, he thought. He hadn't heard a sound out of him for nearly an hour.

The kitchen was gloomy. The dim light over the stove accented the dark corners of the room. Looking for a snack, John Thomas opened the pantry and found a package of Oreos. The box was nearly empty; there were only two broken cookies left. Munching on them, he opened the basement door.

He had planned to go down and get the putty he needed to repair his robot, but when he switched on the light over the basement stairs, the single bulb hissed and went out.

A stale puff of basement air blew into his face. Like a breath, he thought. Suddenly, the dark stairway seemed to yawn like a giant throat. Whirling, he ran out of the kitchen and up to his room.

John Thomas pulled on his pajamas, jumped into bed, and turned off the light. The darkness closed in around him. He snuggled under the bedcovers and shut his eyes. Then he heard it: a low sigh moaning up the stairs. A distant sigh that seemed to come from the basement—that seemed to rise from the depths.

There's nothing there, he told himself. Nothing. Nothing at all.

Silence.

Then he heard it again: a sound that might have been the wind—might have been, except for the faint snuffling sound like air sucked into giant, gummy nostrils.

It's not anything, he thought. He could hear it moving, coming up the basement stairs. The door! The basement door. He had left it open.

You can't hide from it. Anywhere.

The snuffling was louder. John Thomas could hear it over the pounding of his heart. A faint skittering sound came then: a sound that something large and scaly would make if it tried to move across a vinyl floor. It was in the kitchen now. It had to be.

A pause and then a low snort as if green and gummy nostrils flared and sniffed the air.

It can smell the chocolate on your breath.

The Oreos! He had eaten Oreos, and before that Dutch chocolate—and he hadn't even brushed his teeth.

It's coming for you in the dark. It's going to eat your face.

Oh, please. Make it go away.

Eyes squeezed shut, he huddled in the bed and tried not to breathe. Then he heard a sharp hiss and something skittered across the nape of his neck.

John Thomas thought his heart would stop.

The hiss came again. And the touch on his neck became the prod and poke of a finger. "Wake up," came a whisper. "I heard something."

It was Billy. Whirling toward him in a tangle of bedclothes, John Thomas felt his heart start again and bang against his chest. "What? Where?" But he knew the answer. Billy had heard it too. The monster was coming for both of them.

"I'm scared." Billy's whisper shivered into his ear. "It's gonna get me."

John Thomas tried to say, "No it's not," but his voice died in his throat. The skittering sound from the kitchen changed to a low thump-bump. The stairs! It was coming up the stairs!

"It's gonna eat my face."

John Thomas could smell the toothpaste on Billy's breath and underneath the faint sweet smell of . . . chocolate. He leaped out of bed. "It can smell us," he whispered. "We've got to hide." But where? Where? He stared wildly around in the dark. "Under the bed." But even as he said it, he knew that the monster would find them there. It would spread its awful green and gummy nostrils and sniff and know where they were hiding.

"What's it want?"

Us, he thought. It wants us. "We smell like chocolate. And that's what it eats."

A faint sniff—but this time it came from Billy. Then he said, "What if we give it my Oreos?"

"Oreos?" John Thomas's whisper was sharp. "You got Oreos?"

"In my room. I was saving them."

John Thomas thought fast—faster, maybe, than he had ever thought in his life. Billy's room was across the hall, closer to the stairs. Could they make it? But what choice did they have?

Another thump came.

Another.

"Hurry. . . . And be quiet." John Thomas grabbed

Billy's hand, and they were running, bumping in the dark, scurrying across the hall into Billy's room.

The door shut behind them with a little thud. But there was no lock. No lock. No way to keep it out.

The moon made dark shadows stretch across the room. Billy reached for the light switch, but John Thomas grabbed his hand in time. "No, don't!"

Another thump, muffled by the closed door.

"The Oreos. Quick!"

Billy reached under his pillow and brought out a baggie stuffed with the cookies.

John Thomas fumbled inside and pulled out an Oreo. Catching his breath, he moved toward the door and opened it—just a crack. The hall was black and spooky. He strained to listen.

Another thump.

It was near the top of the stairs now. Another step and it would be in the hall.

Clutching the bag of cookies, John Thomas summoned all his courage and ran into the hall to the head of the stairs.

Another thump.

It had to work. Had to work. Had to. He flung the cookie down the stairs and darted back into Billy's room.

Door open just a crack, the boys pressed close together and listened.

A low snuffling groan . . .

Thump-bump.

Thump-bump.

Not daring to move, they clung together in the dark.

Thump-bump.

It was going down the stairs.

Thump-bump.

It *was*. . . .

And then a faint but unmistakable *crunching* sound came from the bottom of the stairs.

"It's got the Oreo," Billy whispered. "Give it another one. Quick. Before it comes back."

They scurried into the hall. Just as the crunching stopped, John Thomas pitched another cookie down the stairs.

The Oreo landed on the floor and slid across the vinyl.

Thump-bump.

A slithering, scraping sound . . .

Crunch.

"Come on. We've got to follow it." Heart racing in his chest, John Thomas crept down the stairs toward the faint blue fluorescent glow coming from the kitchen. Not daring to show his face, he stretched out his arm and pitched another cookie straight toward the basement door.

The boys pressed hard against the wall of the stairway. The baggie felt clammy in John Thomas's hand. There were just two cookies left. Just two.

Scrape-thud.

Scrape-thud.

Scrape-thud.

It was by the basement door now, he was sure.

Crunch.

John Thomas grabbed for a cookie. The basement stairs. He had to throw it down the basement stairs. Then he could shut the door. And lock it. He reached out—and gasped in horror. The cookie popped out of his hand, fell no more than three feet away, and rolled behind the breakfast bar.

Scrape-thud.

Oh no.

Scrape-thud.

It was coming back!

Scrape-thud.

C-R-U-N-C-H.

Just one cookie left. Just one. Just one.

John Thomas darted into the kitchen and flung the last Oreo down the basement stairs.

Then as something—something awful—scuffled behind the breakfast bar, he scurried back to the darkness of the stairs.

Silence.

Thick, awful silence.

And then a dreadful, blood-curdling, snuffling snort.

Scrape-thud.

Scrape-thud.

Ka-bump, ka-bump, ka-bump.

It was going away, down the basement stairs. It was. It was.

Crunch.

John Thomas raced toward the awful basement stairs, grabbed the doorknob, and slammed. The door clicked shut. He scrabbled with the catch; he heard it lock.

"Is it gone?" came Billy's whisper.

John Thomas stared at the basement door.

A faint ka-bump.

Ka-bump, ka-bump.

He shook his head. "It's still there."

"Maybe it can flatten out," said Billy in a low voice. "Maybe it can come under the door."

And the cookies were gone.

"Can it, John Thomas?" Billy began to cry. "What are we gonna do?"

Chocolate, thought John Thomas. It was chocolate the monster was after—and boys who smelled like chocolate. "We've got to get rid of the smell." He flung open the pantry cabinet and stared inside. Then he knew what to do. He grabbed down a can, and then another. "A spoon. Get one quick."

Ka-bump, ka-bump.

With hands that shook, he grabbed the can opener, cranked it, and thrust the open can toward Billy. "Eat it quick." Then he was opening the second can and grabbing a spoon.

"Yuck! It's spinach!"

"Shut up and eat." With frantic haste, John Thomas

dug his spoon into the second can and gobbled. His was beets.

"Uck."

"Eat or you die," said John Thomas with his mouth full.

Ka-bump.

B-U-R-P. . . .

And Billy ate. He ate a half a can of spinach in two bites and the other half in two more. And John Thomas gobbled a can of beets in no time flat.

And they were cold, and nasty, and altogether disgusting. But he didn't care.

They left the empty cans and dirty spoons right there on the countertop and ran upstairs. And they jumped into John Thomas's bed—both of them did—and huddled together.

"Are we okay now?" asked Billy—and his breath was a reassuring spinachy breath.

"I think so," said John Thomas. But then he heard a sound: He heard a scrabbling click and then a metal sound like a lock turning. His heart jumped up in his throat. Then he heard—footsteps.

And it was Daddy. Daddy coming home.

"I think we're okay now," John Thomas said.

And Billy yawned because it was so late and said, "Do you think we can ever eat chocolate again, John Thomas?"

"Maybe," he said, "and maybe not." He snuggled down deep into the covers next to his brother. And the last thing he thought before he went to sleep was: It isn't so bad, really, having to share a room with old Billy.

There are worse things.

3
Baba Yaga and the Sorcerer's Son

by Patricia A. McKillip

Long ago, in a vast and faraway country, there lived a witch named Baba Yaga. She was sometimes very wise and sometimes very wicked, and she was so ugly mules fainted at the sight of her. Most of the time she dwelled in her little house in the deep woods. Occasionally, she dipped down Underearth as easily as if the earth were the sea and the sea were air: down to the World Beneath the Wood.

One morning when she was vacationing Underground, she had an argument with her house, which was turning itself around and around on its chicken legs and wouldn't stop. Baba Yaga, who had stepped outside to find a plump morsel of something for breakfast, couldn't get back in her door. She had given her house chicken legs to cause wonder and consternation in passersby. Nobody was around now but Baba Yaga, her temper simmering like a soup pot, and yet there it was, turning and swaying on its great bony legs in the greeny, underwater light of Underearth, looking for all the world like a demented chicken watching a beetle run circles around it.

"Stop that!" Baba Yaga shouted furiously. "Stop that at once!" Then she made her voice sweet and said the words that you are supposed to say if you come across her house unexpectedly in the forest, and are brave or foolish or desperate enough to want in: "Little house, turn your back to the trees, and open your door to me." But the house, bewildered perhaps by being surrounded by trees, continued turning and turning. Baba Yaga scolded it until her voice was hoarse and flapped her apron at it as if it really were a chicken. "You stupid house!" she raged, for she still hadn't had her breakfast, or even her morning tea. And then, if that wasn't bad enough, the roof of the world opened up at that moment and hurled something big and dark down at her that missed her by inches.

She was so startled the warts nearly jumped off her nose. She peered down at it, blinking, fumbling in her apron for her spectacles.

A young man lay at her feet. He had black hair and black eyelashes; he was dressed in a dark robe with little bits of mirrors and star dust and cat hairs all over it. He looked dead, but as she stared, a little color came back into his waxen face. His eyes fluttered open.

He gave a good yell, for Baba Yaga at her best caused strong windows to crack and fall out of their frames. Baba Yaga lifted her foot and kicked at a huge chicken foot that threatened to step on him, and he yelled again. By then he had air back in his lungs. He rolled and crouched, staring at the witch and trembling.

Then he took a good look at the house. "Oh," he sighed, "it's you, Baba Yaga." He felt himself: neck bone, shin bone. "Am I still alive?"

"Not for long," Baba Yaga said grimly. "You nearly squashed me flat."

He was silent then, huddled in his robe, eyeing her warily. *Baba Yaga*, mothers said to their children in the world above, *will eat you if you don't eat your supper*. He, unimpressed with the warning, had always fed his peas to the dog anyway. And now look. Here she was as promised, payment for thousands of uneaten peas. Baba Yaga's green, prismed glasses glittered at him like a fly's eyes. He bowed his head.

"Oh, well," he said. "If you don't kill me, my father will. I just blew up his house."

Baba Yaga's spectacles slid to the end of her nose. She said grumpily, "Was it spinning?"

"No. It was just sitting there, being a house, with all its cups in the cupboard, and the potatoes growing eyes in the bin, and dust making fuzzballs under the bed, just doing what houses do—"

"Ha!"

"And I was just . . . experimenting a little, with some magic in the cauldron. Baba Yaga, I swear I did exactly what the Book said to do, except we ran out of Dragon root, so I tossed in some Mandragora root instead—I thought it'd be a good substitute—but . . ." His black eyes widened at the memory. "All of a sudden bricks and boards and I went flying, and here I . . . here I . . . Where am I, anyway?"

"Underground."

"Really?" he whispered without sound. "I blew myself that far. Why," he added a breath later, distracted, "is your house doing that?"

"I don't know."

"Well, isn't—doesn't that make it difficult for you to get in the door?"

"Yes."

"Well, then, why are you letting it— When you talk through your teeth like that, does that mean you're angry?"

Baba Yaga shrieked like a hundred boiling tea-kettles. The young man's head disappeared. The house continued to spin.

The witch caught her breath. She felt a little better, and there was the matter of the Sorcerer's son's missing head to contemplate. She waited. A wind full of pale colors and light voices sighed through the trees. She smelled roses from somewhere, maybe from a dream somebody was having about the Underwood. The head emerged slowly, like a turtle's head, from the neck of

the dark robe. The young man looked pale again, uneasy, but his eyes held a familiar, desperate glint.

"Baba Yaga. You must help me. I'll help you."

She snorted. "Do what? Blow my house up?"

"No. Please. You're terrible and capricious, but you
know things. You can help me. Down here, rules blur
into each other. A dream is real; a word spoken here
makes a shape in the world above. If you could just
make things go backward, just for a few moments,
back to the moment before I reached for the Mandragora root—before I destroyed my father's house—if it
could just be whole again—"

"Bosh," Baba Yaga said rudely. "You would blow it
up all over again."

"Would I?"

"Besides, what do you think I am? I can't even get
my house to stop spinning, and you want me to unspin
the world."

He sighed. "Then what am I to do? Baba Yaga, I
love my father and I'm very sorry I blew up his house.
Isn't there anything I can do? I just— Everything is
gone. All his sorcery books, all his lovely precious jars
and bottles, potions and elixirs, his dragon tooth, his
giant's thumbnail, his narwhal tusk—even his five-
hundred-year-old cauldron blew into bits. Not to men-
tion the cups, the beds, his favorite chair, and his
cats—if I landed down here, they probably flew clear
to China. Baba Yaga, he loves me, I know, but if I
were him I might turn me into a toad or something

for a couple of months— Maybe I should just run away to sea. Please?"

Baba Yaga felt momentarily dizzy, as if all his babbling were sailing around her head. She said crossly, "What could you possibly do? I don't want my wood stove and my tea towels blown to China."

"I promise, I promise. . . ." The young man got to his feet, stood blinking at the house twirling precariously on its hen legs among the silent, blue-black trees. It was an amazing sight, one he could tell his children and his grandchildren about if he managed to stay alive that long. *When I was a young man, I fell off the world, down, down to the Underneath, where I met the great witch Baba Yaga. She needed help and only I could help her. . . .*

"Little house," he called. "Little house, turn your back to the trees and open your door to me."

The house turned its feet forward, nestled down like a hen over an egg, opened its door, and stopped moving.

Baba Yaga opened her mouth and closed it, opened her mouth and closed it, looking, for a moment, like the ugliest fish in the world. "How did you—how did you—"

The young man shrugged. "It always works in the stories."

Baba Yaga closed her mouth. She shoved her glasses back up her nose and gave the young man, and then the house, an icy, glittering-green glare. She marched into her house without a word and slammed the door.

"Baba Yaga!" the young man cried. "Please!"

A terrible noise rumbled through the trees then. It was thunder; it was an earthquake; it was a voice so loud it made the grass flatten itself and turn silvery, as under a wind. The young man, his robe puffed and tugged every direction, was blown like a leaf against the side of the house.

"Johann!" the voice said. "Johann!"

The young man squeaked.

The wind died. Baba Yaga's head sprang out of her door like a cuckoo in a clock. "NOW WHAT!"

The young man, trembling again, his face white as tallow, gave a whistle of awe. "My father."

Baba Yaga squinted Upward from behind her prisms. She gave a sharp, decisive sniff, took her spectacles off. Then she took her apron off. She disappeared inside once more. When she came out again, she was riding her mortar and pestle.

The young man goggled. Baba Yaga's house slowly turning on its chicken legs among the trees was an astonishing sight indeed. But Baba Yaga whisking through the air in the bowl she used to grind garlic, rapping its side briskly with the pestle as if it were a horse, made the young sorcerer so giddy he couldn't even tell if the mortar had grown huge, or if Baba Yaga had suddenly gotten very small.

"Come!" she shouted, thrusting a broom handle over the side. He caught it; she pulled him up, dumped him on the bottom of the bowl, and yelled to the mortar, "Geeee-ha!"

Off they went.

It was a wondrous ride. The mortar was so fast it left streaks in the air, which the young man swept away, like clouds, with the broom. Each time he swept he saw a different marvel, far below, like another piece of the rich tapestry of the Underwood. He saw twelve white swans light on a stone in the middle of a darkening sea and turn into princes. He saw an old man standing on a cliff, talking to a huge flounder with a crown on its head. He saw two children, lost in a wood, staring hungrily at the sweet gingerbread house of another witch. He saw a princess in a high tower unbraid her hair and shake it loose so that it tumbled down and down the wall like a river of gold to the bottom, where her true love caught it in his hands. He saw a great, silent palace surrounded by brambles thick as a man's wrist, sharp as daggers, and he saw the King's son who rode slowly toward them. He saw rose gardens and deep, dark forests with red dragons lurking in them. He saw hummingbirds made of crystal among trees with leaves of silver and pearls. He saw secret, solitary towers rising out of the middle of lovely lakes, or from the tops of mountain crags. He whispered, enchanted, as every sweep of the broom filled his eyes with wonders, "There is more magic here than in all my father's books. . . . I could stay here. . . . Maybe I'll stay here. . . . I will stay. . . ." He saw a small pond with a fish in it, as gold as the sun, that spoke once every hundred years. It rose up to the surface as he passed. Its eyes were blue fire; its mouth was full of delicate bubbles like a precious hoard of words. It broke the surface, leaped into the light. It said—

"Johann!"

The mortar bucked in the air like a boat on a wave. The young man sat down abruptly. Baba Yaga said irritably to the sky, "Stop shouting, he's coming. . . ."

"Baba Yaga," the young sorcerer whispered. "Baba Yaga." Still sprawled at the bottom of the mortar, he gripped the hem of her skirt. "Where are you taking me?"

"Home."

"I stopped—" he whispered, for his voice was gone. "I stopped your house. I helped you."

"Indeed," the witch said. "Indeed you did. But I am Baba Yaga, and no one ever knows from one moment to the next what I will do."

She said nothing more. The young man slumped over himself, not even seeing the Firebird below, with her red beak and diamond eyes, stealing golden apples from the garden of the King. He sighed. Then he sighed again. Then he said, with a magnificent effort, "Oh, well. I suppose I can stand to leave all this behind and be a toad for a few months. It's as much as I deserve. Besides, if I ran away, he'd miss me." He stood up then, and held out his arms to the misty, pastel sky of the world within the World. "Father! It's me! I'm coming back. I'm coming . . ."

Baba Yaga turned very quickly. She rapped the young sorcerer smartly on the head with her pestle. His eyes closed. She caught him in her arms as he swayed, and she picked him up and tossed him over the side of the mortar. But instead of falling down, he fell up, up into the gentle, opalescent sky, up until Up was Down below the feet of those who dwelled in the world Above.

"And good riddance," Baba Yaga said rudely. But she lingered in her mortar to listen.

"Oh," the young sorcerer groaned. "My head."

"Johann! You're alive!"

"Barely. That old witch Baba Yaga hit me over the head with her pestle—"

"Hush, don't talk. Rest."

"Father, is that you? Am I here?"

"Yes, yes, my son—"

"I'm sorry I blew up your house."

"House, shmouse, you blew up your head, you stupid boy, how many times have I told you—"

"It was the Mandragora root."

"I know. I've told you and told you—"

"Is this my bed? The house is still standing? Father, your cauldron, the cats, the pictures on the wall—"

"Nothing is broken but your head."

"Then I didn't— But how did I— Father, I blew myself clear to the Underwood—I saw Baba Yaga's house spinning and spinning, and I stopped it for her,

and she took me for a ride in her mortar and pestle—
I saw such wonders, such magics, such a beautiful
country. . . . Someday I'll find my way back. . . ."

"Stop talking. Sleep."

"And then she hit me for no reason at all, after I
had helped her, and she sent me back here. . . . Did
you know she wears green spectacles?"

"She does not!"

"Yes, she does."

"You were dreaming."

"Was I? Was I, really? Or am I dreaming now that
the house is safe, and you aren't angry. . . . Which is
the true dream?"

"You're making my head spin."

"Mine, too."

The voices were fading. Baba Yaga smiled, and three
passing crows fell out of the sky in shock. She beat a
drumroll on the mortar with her pestle and sailed back
to her kitchen.

4

All the Names of Baby Hag

by Patricia MacLachlan

Listen. Do you hear it? That soft wet sound when the waves come in and slide back again? It is the whisper of the sea hags, soft and sly. An every-so-often whisper as they come up from the sea and disguise themselves—a rest from the tiresome peace under the water, the boring rise and fall, in and out of the tides. You have seen the hags, yes you have, don't shake your head. The leather-faced, chicken-legged women with gold chains yelling, "Stop throwing sand, Dwight. This very minute. I meeean it!" Sea hags. The old man with the bucket belly who sleeps with his face to the sun, mouth open, awakening suddenly with a drool. A sea hag. The silent child who visits your beach blanket and eats up your french fries before you notice. Sea hag.

* * *

Baby Sea Hag was born in the stillness of a slack
tide. She was round and the pale-green color of a sea
urchin, with delicate diaphanous fins and tidy webbed
feet.

"Lovely hag," Mother Hag murmured. "Like the
others."

Father Hag nodded, his long whiskers trailing in the
sea. Baby Hag reached out to touch one.

"I wonder what she will choose for her name," mused
Father Hag.

"She will find the special name, all her own, just for
her," said Mother Hag. "All sea hags do, after all. She
will, too."

Baby Hag's brothers and sisters, dozens of them,
came from the eel grasses and tidal pools and marshes
to see her. They filled the water with breath bubbles
that brushed her nose and made her sneeze. Like Baby
Hag they were all perfect and pale-green-round, with
fins and webbed feet. But Baby Hag was different.
She smiled from the moment she was born, for one
thing. And she laughed out loud before a full day had
passed, unusual for hags. They are generally purposeful and serious-minded creatures. Not frivolous.
Certainly not cheerful on a daily basis.

"All the time she's happy!" exclaimed Baby Hag's
sister, Snow White Hag. She had found her name when
she was disguised as a child, sitting on the edge of a
blanket with other children. She had listened to tales

read from a book, eating soft white-bread sandwiches with the crusts cut off, seven sweet pickles, and the last lemon sour ball. She had loved that story of human creatures and the sound of the two words that would become her name. The two words that meant the same. Snow. White.

"I thought she was your sister," one boy complained to the other after she'd gone.

"Mine! Isn't she *yours?* She ate all the pickles!"

Rex, the oldest of the hag children, swam in circles while Baby Hag trailed behind. "Special she may be," he said, "but she will have to find her own name the way we all did. Up on the land." Rex had spent one lively morning with a large loping black Labrador whose tag read: *Rex is ours. Send him home. We love him.* Rex had loved the dog's sweet, sloppy nature. He had taken him home. And at the end of the day slipped back to the sea with his name.

"Land is far better than the sea for names," said Beach Pea shyly. "Nothing is nameless on land. Children, buildings—humans often name their houses, do you believe it?—and their boats!" Often, when the blooms came, Beach Pea went up to the shore, disguised as a toad or a child, a sand flea or a grandmother, to peer at the pink-lavender bloom of the beach pea. "Even cars they name," she added. "Chevrolet. Chev-ro-lay. Lovely, don't you think, Chevrolet?"

Baby Hag smiled.

"She likes it!" cried Beach Pea.

"She does," said Mother Hag, matter-of-factly. "She likes Mirabelle, Clothilde, and Veronica, too. And Baby Bernice."

"All of them?" asked Father Hag, amazed.

"All of them."

"What about Olivia?" suggested Beach Pea. "I met an Olivia once when I was a hungry human standing in line for a hamburger."

"Ah, hamburger," said Father Hag softly, remembering his time ashore. He had taken the form of a parking attendant. "I once ate seven. Odd things, hamburgers."

"Mirabelle?"

"Clothilde?"

"Veronica?"

Baby Hag smiled at the names.

"Olivia?"

"Hamburger?" Father Hag's suggestion.

Baby Hag smiled.

"Pippit? A lively and restless name."

"Grandma Meeker? She fished at night by lantern light."

"Elizabeth Margaret Bernadette Mary O'Shaughnessy? She was very bad mannered. She licked all the sandwiches and had to sit the afternoon on a towel."

Still Baby Hag smiled.

"She likes all the names," said Mother Hag. "Strange. Or worse, unnatural."

Father Hag touched Baby Hag very lightly with a

fin. "She likes one name as well as another, it seems," he said.

And she did. So the other young hags, the dozens of brothers and sisters, all of them generally purposeful and serious-minded hags, went back to their generally purposeful and serious-minded lives. And Baby Hag did not have a name. She didn't have one name, that is. She answered to any and all names. Names that the sea hags had heard on land, crouched in the dune grass, listening; lying on beach blankets, pretending sleep; standing in food lines with handfuls of human food with the strange names. *Onion ring. Chili dog. Submarine. Shake.*

Each day Mother Hag tried out new names.

"Dilly?"

"What?"

"Trixie?"

"Here I am."

"Cousin Coot!"

"Coming!"

"This is impossible," said Mother Hag, crossly. "There is no living hag without a name. Never in hag history has there been a nameless hag!"

"There is now," said Father Hag very softly.

"It cannot go on," said Mother Hag. "It will not go on!"

But it did. The tides rose and fell with magical monotony, and Baby Hag rose and fell, slept and wakened with them. She was left with the lovely light of the sea at dawn, and the dark of it at night. With no names. With *all* names. *Melissa, Sandcastle, Nanny, Umbrella, Myna, Sunrise* . . .

One season led to another—autumn to winter with dark seas and wind, and the rumble of rocks beneath the waves. *Gloria, Alice-Iris, Zoë, Aunt Zell, Sunset* . . .

Not many creatures roamed the land when it was winter; only someone walking now and then, a dog or two or three, and the raccoons at nighttime. Once there was a kite flyer, high in the dunes, and Snow White Hag went up to ask her name. One moment there was nothing but sea and rocks and a great wave. The next moment there was a small, pale child bundled up against the cold.

"My name? Doodoo Schwartz the Third," the kite flyer told Snow White Hag without looking. "*Doo* Schwartz the Third for short." Above, the kite whirled and dipped and fluttered in the winter wind. When she looked again to see who'd asked for her name there was no child. *No child at all.*

"Doodoo Schwartz is nice," Baby Hag told Snow White Hag. "Third is nice, too." She swam in circles, upside down, so that the late sunlight warmed her pale underbelly. "All nice."

"She *is* different, Baby Hag is," said one hag to another. "Liking all those names, not one her own . . . and all that cheer!"

"She will change," said Mother Hag, worried.

"Maybe," said Father Hag. He did not look worried, but he was. Sea hags, purposeful and serious minded, always worried.

Winter turned to spring and spring to summer, with the great warm sea surrounding Baby Hag. Father Hag watched Baby Hag closely. He swam with the currents, Baby Hag following always, and went about his life thinking about names. He thought very hard, as if one name—just one name of all the names—might float like a bubble into Baby Hag's mind. Or heart. *Lucy, Chloe, Afton, Wild Annie . . .*

Rex went up to land as a beagle, his face to the ground, sniffing out names like a dog nosing for food. Beach Pea went, too, though no one knew what form she took. She visited a garden.

"How about Runner Bean?" she suggested. "Or Rosa Ragosa—wild blooms by the sea. Or . . ." She swam close to whisper to Baby Hag, "Eggplant! Luminous during the full moon, and firm bodied."

Baby Hag liked Luminous.

Rex returned breathless after two days. He had raced the beaches and sea roads with two dogs, in and out of the wild honeysuckle, up and down the dunes, back and forth through steaming compost heaps; sending up flocks of quail, chasing cats whose hair stood in ridges along their backs. At dusk chewing on old bones.

Rex sighed and treaded water wearily.

"A waste of time," he announced. "One was a

tiresome terrier whose name you wouldn't want. The small one was too low to the ground and had a flat forehead. Lady? Scruffy?"

Baby Hag shook her head.

Snow White Hag sighed.

"You must have a name," she said sadly. "A name that means you."

"*My* name means me," said Beach Pea thoughtfully. "Sometimes, just before sleep, I think about the color of the wild blooms against the sand. And the soft feel of them."

"I think about Rex on land even in daylight," said Rex. "I see him in the eye of my mind stalking cars, rolling by the water in the carcass of a dead cod; twitching his legs in his dreams."

"I know," said Baby Hag, nodding her head up and down. "Lots of names mean me. All names. If I have one name, you know, I cannot have another. If I am Veronica I can't be Eggplant. And if I come when you call Clothilde I can't when you call Pippit."

"No," said Mother Hag fiercely. "I am weary of this. It is not the way of hags. One hag, one name. And that is that!"

There was a silence that grew slowly like the full-moon tide filling a marsh. Even Rex, sometimes as easygoing as a mutt, was silent and serious.

"The first fair day," said Mother Hag firmly, "you will go up to land and find a name. There will be a long, warm shore full of names."

"Many names," agreed Baby Hag cheerfully. "All names."

At this Mother Hag lost all reason.

"Not all names!" she cried. With every word a burst of bubbles came forth. "The first name you hear. *That* will be your name. Then you will return to the sea and we'll all live in peace." She looked at Baby Hag and her face softened a bit. "And you will have one name. One name that means you."

The sun had faded long ago. Night moved overhead, and slowly, without a word, the other hags swam off. They would return with the sun.

One name. Only one name Mother Hag wanted for Baby Hag; Baby Hag wished for all names. Impossible. One name. All names. It became a song that sang in Father Hag's head, over and over. He closed his eyes and rocked gently in the sea. One name. All names. *The first name she heard.* Impossible. *Or was it?* Suddenly Father Hag opened his eyes in the darkness. He smiled. It was strange to him, the smiling, though it felt familiar like a sudden smell from the past, a glimpse of something nearly, but not quite, forgotten. The night rains came, and the soft dropping on the water finally lulled him to sleep. He smiled all through his dreams.

Morning bloomed bright. There were dogs by the sea, and children with their pants rolled, chasing waves.

"Now," Mother Hag said to Baby Hag. "Quickly before the other hag children come. Go up to land for your name."

Father Hag smiled at Baby Hag and nodded his head.

Baby Hag peered at him. There was something. Something about his eyes that made her smile, too.

"Will you come with me?" she asked.

Father Hag shook his head.

"You will be fine. Remember, the first name you hear."

Baby Hag nodded, and with a quick flash of fin she swam to the surface of the sea. Into the first rise of wave she went, over and onto the next, and to the next. Six waves she rode, and then, with a great rush of foam and rolling wave and the barest whisper of sound, she tumbled onto wet sand—a small child blinking in the sunlight. It was strange on land, warm and bright. There was no safe darkness of the sea, no brothers and sisters. For the first time she felt earth beneath her feet.

Nearby sat a child, building a sand castle, humming to herself; another was throwing sand; a mother asleep, a father calling. Baby Hag turned around with a start, and there stood a child staring at her. The child's hair was short, and it was hard to tell if it was a boy child or girl. The child moved closer, closer, until it stood a breath away, arms folded, a small string of jingle shells strung in a bracelet on one wrist. Baby Hag tried to look away. But there was something about the child's eyes. Suddenly the child reached out and touched Baby Hag lightly, very lightly, and the string of jingle shells made a soft sweet noise. *Something about the eyes.* Baby Hag stared at the child. She took a deep breath. And she spoke.

"What is your name?"

She had never heard her own voice out of the sea. It seemed to fly away like spindrift.

The child smiled.

"Guess," said the child.

Guess.

In that moment the wind died and there was a great stillness between one wave and another. Baby Hag smiled at the child. And with a small sound, with the next wave, Baby Hag was gone.

"Was that a child?" called a woman nearby, looking alarmed. "Where did that child go?"

A man shook his head.

"Who was she? What was her name?"

They both turned to ask the other child. But the other child was gone, too. *There was no child at all.*

Her name? Baby Hag heard the question and swam wave past wave past wave, slipping down again through the cool waters of her home. Down where her family waited for her.

"What is it?" called Rex, excited.

"Your name?" asked Mother Hag.

Baby Hag smiled at them.

"Guess," she said.

"Clothilde?"

"Martine?"

"No," said Baby Hag, shaking her head. "Guess."

"Lila?"

"Lizzie?"

A slight brush of fins touched Baby Hag then, and her father was there beside her.

"She has told you her name," he said. "It is not Clothilde or Francine, Lila or Lizzie. Her name," he said slowly, "is Guess."

There was a silence. Rex was the first to speak.

"Guess," he said. He laughed. "Guess."

"One name," said Mother Hag softly.

"One name for those who know her," said Father Hag. "But from those who ask her, she will always hear all the names she loves."

Baby Hag . . . Guess . . . turned to look at Father Hag, and she smiled suddenly at what she saw. Around one fin, so delicate that it moved in the currents of the water, hung a string of white jingle shells.

There it is, that whisper again! Hush, and you may hear another. It may be a child who appears suddenly, silently behind you, or a dog who grins. If the dog follows you, quickly tell him your name and he will trot away. If the child asks your name, do not say Guess. There is already a Guess who smiles and dreams beneath the sea. She lives with the lovely light of the sea at dawn, and the dark of it at night. With one name. With all names. And one thing more. Around her neck she wears a slim thread necklace of jingle shells.

5
The Three Men

by Zilpha Keatley Snyder

Guy was way up in the pepper tree when the three
men came over the ridge. He'd climbed up there right
after he dropped Aunt's favorite platter because he
needed time to decide what to do; whether to tell her
and get it over with, or run away a year early. He'd
always planned to wait until he was twelve, but then
that heavy old platter that Aunt set such great store
by had to go and slip out of his soapy hands. After
he'd swept up the pieces and hid them in the ash pile
he'd climbed the pepper tree. He cried some, but the
wind that had been blowing all day long dried his tears
before he could even taste them.

After a while he stopped crying and stretched out
with his cheek on the prickly bark. He wrapped his
arms and legs around the thick limb and hung on tightly

while the Santa Ana, the hot, dry wind blowing in from the desert, dried his eyes and whisked long strands of pepper leaves, like thin prickly fingers, across his face and arms. Hanging on like that made him feel better. It wasn't that he was afraid of falling. It was just a good feeling to be almost a part of the solid old tree.

The sun had gone down and the sky behind the razorback ridge turned fiery red before Aunt came home from town. The first thing Guy heard was the clip clop of hooves, and for a moment he prayed that it might be Juliet, Uncle Joe's riding mare. But he might have known it wasn't. Uncle Joe had gone to the Gardners' to help with the new barn, and there was to be a shindig afterward that would probably last until late at night. Aunt had done a lot of yelling that morning when Uncle Joe said he was going to the barn raising. She'd said it was just like him to go off and waste a whole day helping riffraff like the Gardners while there was so much that needed doing right there on their own place.

Among a whole lot of other things, she'd also yelled that she was leaving. She was going off to Pasadena, she said, to live with her rich sister. But Guy hadn't gotten his hopes up. She was always saying that, and she never did go. But this time after Uncle Joe left, Aunt told Guy to harness up Old Jacob, and for a moment he'd wondered. But then she'd said she was only going into town to buy a length of dress goods.

And now it was sunset, and the hooves in the driveway were Old Jacob's, and a few minutes later Guy heard the squeaky groan of the buggy as Aunt climbed out. Not long afterward she came out on the kitchen stoop and called.

"Guy! You Guy!" she yelled four or five times before she gave up and went back into the house. So far she was probably only wanting him to come take care of Old Jacob. She sounded angry but no more than usual, so she hadn't noticed the missing platter yet. Guy was thinking he had to hurry up and decide, and starting to cry all over again, when he looked up—and there they were.

There were three of them, and against the smoky red of the sky they looked as dark and crookedy as burnt matchsticks. They came slowly up above the horizon, their spiky elbows and knees bending like rusty hinges. They went on walking right up the ridge for a ways, jiggling along like puppet toys on a stage, before they started down through the high pasture. At first Guy was too busy worrying about Aunt and the platter to think much about them. It crossed his mind that they were probably some of the Jacksons on their way home from the Gardners' shindig. It took them a long time to disappear into the gully in the west fork and an even longer time to come back into sight on the other side, and in the meantime Guy had other things to think about.

Aunt came out again and yelled, and from in front

of the house Guy could hear Old Jacob nickering and thumping the ground with a front hoof, eager to be taken to the barn and rubbed down and fed. Guy had almost forgotten about the three men, wondering what to do about Old Jacob and Aunt and the platter, when all of a sudden there they were again. Now that they were nearer and below the sunset he could see flutters of raggedy clothing and long gray wisps of hair that blew back from beneath the broad brims of their hats. Seeing them in the red-stained dusk and especially from behind a fringe of pepper leaves, a person might have taken them for road-weary travelers, or three old prospectors down from the high mountains. Guy might have climbed down from the tree and gone to meet them, if he hadn't remembered, all of a sudden, about something Violet had told him way back last winter.

Violet lived on a big rackety homestead in Dry Barranca Valley with George and Amelia Gardner, who were her father and mother. There'd been a lot of other flowers, Rose and Lily and maybe even Geranium and Petunia, but they'd all gotten married and left home before Violet was born. Aunt said the Gardners should have quit trying for George Herbert Gardner Junior after the fifth or sixth flower. Aunt said she'd told Amelia Gardner as much, right to her face. But according to Aunt, Amelia Gardner wasn't one to listen to well-meant advice, and they'd gone ahead and tried again for a boy. And all they got was Violet. Aunt said that Violet was what came of having a young'un when you were old enough to be its grandma. Aunt said Violet was loony.

Guy didn't know. He liked listening to Violet. Maybe it was loony and maybe it was plain fibbing, but whatever it was he liked hearing it. "Hey, Violet!" he'd yell when he saw her at recess or on her way to school, and she'd stop and wait for him, with her sparky eyes glittering and a secret smile tightening the corners of her mouth. "Hey," he'd say again and she'd start right in telling him one thing or another. Nothing Violet told him was like the kind of things most people talked about, but Guy didn't know if it was loony or not.

Some of it was about dragons. That was when Guy first started going to Barranca School after somebody wrote to the county (Aunt said it was probably Amelia Gardner that did it), and the truant officer came and had a long talk with Aunt. That year Guy and Violet and Nellie Anderson were the whole fourth grade, only Guy was ten already and would have been in the fifth if the truant officer had come sooner.

After the dragons it was unicorns for a while. Once when Aunt had gone into town, Guy had gone with Violet to look for one in the clearing near the Joneses' spring. He hadn't seen anything but an old hoof mark that looked like it might have been made by the Joneses' billygoat. But Violet had seen the unicorn. That's what she said, anyway.

But then, after Violet started visiting with Old Sally,

she began to talk about other things besides unicorns and dragons. Old Sally had lived in the shanty near the sawmill since before most folks could remember. Some of the church ladies took her food now and then, but no one ever talked to her much except Violet. Old Sally told Violet about things like ghosts and haunts and spirits, and all about the three men. And then Violet told Guy.

That was when Guy stopped going to the outhouse for a while. Actually, he hadn't much liked going out there after dark, even before he heard about the three men. Like when Violet told him about the Paulsons' dead baby that Old Sally heard crying in the cemetery, and another time about how her cat wouldn't go in the back room of her cabin because somebody had died there. But after he heard about the three men there was a spell when he just couldn't go out into the dark anymore, past the woodshed with its open door and the shadowy rows of the berry patch. So on dark nights he peed near the back door—until Aunt caught him doing it.

Aunt got out the razor strop right away that time, but then Uncle Joe slowed things down by asking why Guy had been peeing in the ash pile. As soon as he could stop crying enough to talk, Guy told them what Violet had said about the three men, and Uncle Joe said that was enough to make anybody pee in the ash pile. Uncle Joe was like that. Sometimes Guy wished that Uncle Joe was really his uncle except that would make Aunt really his aunt. And the truth was, neither of them was kin at all. Guy just had to pretend they were because of what Aunt told Mrs. Austin at the orphanage. Aunt said she'd come looking for her nephew and she'd found what she was looking for, but part of that wasn't true. The true part was that she found what she was looking for—someone big enough to do a man's work and small enough to be kept in line with a razor strop.

Usually Aunt was as quick with that old strop as Jesse James with a six-shooter, but that time it took her more than half an hour to get around to it. After Guy had told her and Uncle Joe what Violet had said, Aunt just stood there swishing the strop around like a flat blacksnake while she finished the argument with Uncle Joe.

It took a long time even though Uncle Joe didn't get to say very much, as usual. What he did get said was that he'd always thought it was too bad what happened to those three men, and he'd thought so at the time but he'd been too young to do much about it. But Aunt said that was just like him, sticking up for three foreigners against his own kith and kin. And even if they hadn't been the ones who stole the horses, like it turned out, they'd been up to no good, hanging around the valley like that, watching what folks were doing and trying to talk to people they had no business talking to. And the cabin catching fire the way it did when her pa and the rest of the men tried to smoke them out just saved the expense of a trial and three hanging ropes. The argument went on for a long time, but it wasn't long enough to make Aunt forget about what Guy had done—or about using the razor strop. After- ward Guy wondered if she might have forgotten if he'd told her everything Violet had said about the three men.

Up in the pepper tree it all came back sharp and clear, the way Violet had told it. He had time to think about all of it while the three men were still coming down the hill. It wasn't that they were moving so slowly. Their arms and legs swung back and forth so fast their raggedy gray tatters streamed out behind, and from beneath their feet dust whirled back in a twisting white cloud like smoke from a chimney. But they walked and walked and walked, and moved only from one fencepost to the next, as if they were walking forward and at the same time drifting backward on the east wind, like a swimmer going upstream. From behind a shivering fringe of pepper-tree leaves, Guy watched them coming and thought about what Violet had said.

"Old Sally told me they always come out when it's hot and dry with a Santa Ana blowing, the way it did the night it happened. On a hot, dry day they come up out of Grandpa Jackson's grave and start looking."

"What the Sam Hill are they doing in Grandpa Jack- son's grave?" Guy had asked.

"That's where the men put them," Violet said, "because it was handy. Old Sally says that Grandpa Jackson was such a suspicious old coot that he made his kin dig his grave ahead of time so he could be sure they didn't skimp on it. So after the fire, there it was all ready, and that's where they put them. But now and then they come out again and go looking for the ones who did it."

"What would they do if they found any of them?" Guy asked.

"They already have," Violet said, nodding her head very slowly. "They've found them, all right. Some of them."

Guy swallowed hard. "Who—who'd they find?"

"Haven't you ever heard about Frank Appleby?"

"Mr. Appleby's name is Sam," Guy said.

Violet nodded. "Frank was his uncle. He was there that night when the cabin caught fire, and a few years after that his mare threw him one night down by the barranca. She was a lazy old thing he'd been riding for years, and Frank was a real good rider. But he'd a broken neck when they found him."

Guy felt his throat tighten like it did when Aunt got out the razor strop. He didn't like to think about Frank Appleby, or anybody, being alone at night in the wide dry riverbed, with its clumps of willow trees and big dark boulders. Besides, he was pretty sure that Violet was just fibbing again.

"And then there was your aunt's pa. They got him, too," Violet said.

Guy had stared at her until his eyes began to feel dry and bulgy, but then he remembered something. "Nobody got Aunt's pa," he said, grinning with relief. "Aunt says her pa died right there in her house—of pneumonia. I remember her saying it lots of times."

Violet narrowed her eyes and tipped her secret smile into a knowing grin. "Maybe," she said. "And maybe not. Didn't she say how sudden it was? How everybody thought he just had a bad cold and how everybody thought—"

"That he was going to be up and about in a day or two," Guy finished for her, remembering Aunt's exact words. "And then the family all went off to the church picnic, and they stayed late because the weather was so fine and warm, and when they got back—"

Violet nodded. "And when they got back it was too late. And then there was Marybelle Mayberry."

"Marybelle who?" Guy had asked.

"Mayberry. The Mayberrys don't live here anymore. They moved away right after Marybelle disappeared."

"She disappeared?" Guy didn't like to think about disappearing. Just hearing the word made the scalp pucker all the way up the back of his head. Maybe it was because he'd always had a suspicion that there was a kind of belongingness that held people in place and without it there wasn't much to keep you from just waking up one morning and finding out you weren't there. There'd never been a whole lot for Guy to hold on to—not in the orphanage, and not much more in a house that belonged to people who were only pretend kin. And it was knowing that there'd be even less to hang on to when he was all alone and out on the open road that had kept him at Aunt's for so long, in spite of the razor strop. Disappearing was one thing he surely didn't like to hear about.

"Why'd they want to bother Marybelle?" he asked Violet. "There weren't any women at the cabin that night, were there?"

"Not that night. But Marybelle was the reason it happened. One of the reasons anyway. It was two girls who found out that the men were living in the old prospectors' cabin, and the two of them went around telling people about it. And that wasn't all they said."

"What else did they say?" Guy asked. He had a feeling he didn't want to hear any more about it, but he could tell that Violet wanted him to ask, so he did.

Violet rolled her eyes. "Those two girls said they were berrying along the creek bed and when they passed the cabin the men came out and called to them and asked them to come in."

Guy felt uneasy. He'd heard enough talk in the orphanage, the big boys mostly, whispering together out by the back fence, to have an idea why three strange men might ask some girls into their cabin. He had an idea, but he asked anyway. Looking down at his toe poking out through the hole in his left shoe, he asked, "Why'd they do that?"

Violet leaned forward. " 'Marybelle! Birdie!' is what

those men called. 'Come in and have a cup of coffee,' and maybe they went in and maybe they didn't, but then they ran away and told their fathers; but Old Sally says, 'How'd those men know their names if those girls hadn't talked to them before, and maybe been there before and—' "

"Birdie!" Guy said, all of a sudden. "Not Birdie—"

Violet nodded. "*Aunt* Birdie," she said.

Guy gasped. He'd almost forgotten that Aunt's given name was Birdie. Aunt hated her name, and she wouldn't let anybody call her by it, not even Uncle Joe. Guy had seen it written once or twice, but it had taken him a minute or two to remember the writing when Violet had told him how Marybelle and Birdie had been a part of what happened that night at the old prospectors' cabin.

So perhaps the three men had been to Aunt's place once before and perhaps they had reason to come back again, and that was why Guy had been afraid to go outdoors after dark for a while last winter. But when Aunt had caught him peeing in the ash pile he hadn't told her everything. He hadn't mentioned Marybelle or Birdie. He hadn't dared—and besides, he figured he didn't need to. Aunt already knew what Marybelle and Birdie had, or hadn't, done.

The sunset had faded from fire to ash by the time the three men reached the edge of the apricot orchard, and in the deepening shadows it was hard to tell just where they went in, or how. There they were one minute, striding in and out of shadows, and the next minute they were gone; as if the orchard trees had reached out for them and swallowed them up. But even though he couldn't see them anymore he knew they were coming closer and closer, and all he could do was hang on to the pepper tree with all his strength and try to swallow the sound of his thundering heart. And then it was dark.

The Santa Ana was still blowing, and beneath the pepper tree the darkness flowed and moaned. Guy could hear the wavering moan and the hissing whisper of the leaves and nothing more. No sound came from the house or from in front of it where Old Jacob was still waiting at the hitching rail. The blinding flow of darkness was unbroken except where, through a blur of shivering black leaves, three dim squares of light had begun to glow. Lamps had been lit in the kitchen and parlor and in Aunt's bedroom upstairs. Aunt was waiting there, alone, behind the glowing windows, and somewhere in the invisible orchard the three men were striding forward against the dark wind.

Guy loosened his hold on the prickly limb and began to move backward. He'd almost reached the trunk of the tree when a new and larger patch of light shot out across the yard toward the pepper tree. And then Aunt appeared, a black paper woman, long and thin against the lamplight, with a black paper razor strop dangling from her hand. She stood there for a moment, and then she went back in. Guy heard the squeak of door hinges and saw the rectangle of light narrow away to blackness, and then he put his face down again against the peppery bark and closed his eyes. He didn't open them or turn his head when he heard the hinges creak again, and then a second time, and then a third.

Aunt left that night for Pasadena. She must have packed her things and loaded them into the buggy in a hurry, in the dead of night. When Uncle Joe came home she was already gone and so was Old Jacob and the buggy, and the house was in an awful mess. As soon as Uncle Joe found Guy, still hiding in the pepper tree, he showed him how the front door had been left wide open so that the Santa Ana had gotten in and blown out the lamps and scattered papers and dead leaves and all the ashes from the fireplace from one end of the house to the other. They cleaned the whole house early the next morning, but it had gone on smelling of ashes for two or three days.

Guy liked living alone with Uncle Joe. The apricots did very well that year, and in the fall Uncle Joe bought another riding horse and taught Guy how to ride and rope so he'd be ready for when they'd saved up enough money to start their beef herd. And sometimes Violet came over and taught Guy how to cook things that Uncle Joe wasn't very good at. Uncle Joe still didn't talk very much, but what he did say Guy liked to listen to almost as much as he liked to listen to Violet.

They hardly ever talked about Aunt, but once Uncle Joe said he guessed it was the Gardners' barn raising that did it, and if he'd known that was all it would take he'd have built a barn for the Gardners a whole lot sooner, even if he'd had to do it all by himself.

Guy didn't say anything. He never mentioned the three men. And he especially never mentioned the ashes. He never told Uncle Joe or anybody that one of the chores he'd done that day while Aunt was in town was to clean every last sliver of ashes out of the fireplace.

6

Great-Grandfather Dragon's Tale

by Jane Yolen

1

"Long, long ago," said the old dragon, and the gray smoke curled around his whiskers in thin, tired wisps, "in the time of the Great-Grandfather of All Dragons, there was no Thanksgiving."

The five little dragons looked at one another in alarm. The boldest of them, Sskar, said, "No Thanksgiving? No feasting? No chestnuts on the fire? Hasn't there always been a Thanksgiving?"

The old dragon wheezed. The smoke came out in huge, alarming puffs. Then he started speaking, and the smoke resumed its wispy rounds. "For other animals, perhaps. For rabbits or lions or deer. Perhaps for them there has always been a Thanksgiving."

"Rabbits and lions and deer!" The little dragons said the names with disdain. And Sskar added, "Who cares about rabbits and lions and deer. We want to know about dragons!"

"Then listen well, young saurs. For what was once could come again. What was then could be now. And once there was no Dragons' Thanksgiving."

The little dragons drew closer, testing their claws against the stone floor of the cave, and listened.

Long, long ago *began the old dragon* the world was ice and fire, fire and ice. In the south, great mountains rained smoke and spat flame. In the north, glaciers like beasts crept down upon the land and devoured it.

It was then that the Great-Grandfather of All Dragons lived.

He was five hundred slithes from tip to tail. His scales shimmered like the moon on waves. His eyes were as black as shrouds. He breathed fire storms, which he could fan to flame with his mighty wings. And his feet were broad enough to carry him over the thundering miles. All who saw him were afraid.

And the Great-Grandfather of All Dragons ate up the shaking fear of the little animals. He lived on it and thrived. He would roar and claw and snatch and hit about with his tail just to watch fear leap into the eyes of the watchers. He was mighty, yet he was just one of many, for in those days dragons ruled the earth.

One day, up from the south, from the grassy lands, from the sweet lands, where the red sun pulls new life from the abundant soil, a new creature came. He was smaller than the least of the dragons, not even a slithe and a half high. He had no claws. His teeth were puny and blunt. He could breathe neither fire nor smoke, and he had neither armor to protect himself nor fur to keep himself warm. His legs could only carry him from here—to there. *And the old dragon drew a small line on the rockface with his littlest toenail.*

But when he opened his mouth, the sounds of all beasts, both large and small, of the air and the sea and the sky came out. It was this gift of sound that would make him the new king.

"Fah!" said little Sskar. "How could something that puny be a king? The only sound worth making more than once or twice is this." And he put his head back and roared. It was a small roar for he was still a small dragon, but little as it was, it echoed for miles and caused three trees to wither on the mountain's face. True, they were stunted trees that had weathered too many storms and were above the main tree line. But they shivered at the sound, dropped all their remaining leaves, and died where they stood.

The other little dragons applauded the roar, their claws clacketting together. And one of them, Sskitter, laughed. Her laugh was delicate and high pitched, but she could roar as loudly as Sskar.

"*Do not laugh at what you do not understand,*" *said the old dragon.* "*Look around. What do you see? We are few, yet this new creature is many. We live only in this hidden mountain wilderness while he and his children roam the rest of the world. We glide on shrunken wings over our shrunken kingdom while he flies in great silver birds all over the earth.*"

"*Was it not always so?*" *asked the smallest dragon, Sskarma. She was shaken by the old one's words.*

"*No, it was not always so,*" *said the old dragon.*

"*Bedtime,*" *came a soft voice from the corner. Out from behind a large rock slithered Mother Dragon.* "*Settle down, my little fire tongues. And you, Grandfather, no more of that story for this night.*"

"*Tomorrow?*" *begged Sskarma, looking at the old one.*

He nodded his mighty head, and the smoke made familiar patterns around his horns.

As they settled down, the little dragons listened while their mother and the old one sang them a lullaby.

> "*Firelight and firebright,*
>   *Bank your dragon flames tonight.*
>   *Close your eyes and still your roar,*
>   *Sleep is here, my little saur.*
>   *Hiss, hiss, hush.*"

By the time the song was over, all but little Sskar had dropped off. He turned around and around on the cave floor, trying to get settled. "*Fah!*" *he muttered to himself. "What kind of king is that?" But at last he, too, was asleep, dreaming of bones and fire.*

"Do not fill their heads with nonsense," said Mother Dragon when the hatchlings were quiet.

"It is not nonsense," said the old dragon. "It is history."

"It is dreams," she retorted. In her anger, fire shot out of her nostrils and singed the old one's nose. "If it cannot feed their bellies, it is worthless. Good night, Grandfather." She circled her body around the five little dragons and, covering them, slept.

The old dragon looked at the six of them long after the cave was silent. Then he lay down with his mouth open facing the cave entrance as he had done ever since he had taken a mate. He hardly slept at all.

2

In the morning, the five little dragons were up first, yawning and hissing and stretching. They sharpened their claws on the stone walls, and Sskar practiced breathing smoke. None of the others was even close to smoke yet. Most were barely trickling straggles through their nose slits.

It was midmorning before Grandfather Dragon moved. He had been up most of the night thinking, checking the wind currents for scents, keeping alert for dangerous sounds carried on the air. When morning had come, he had moved away from the cave mouth and fallen asleep. When Grandfather awoke it was in sections. First his right foreleg moved, in short hesitations as if testing its flexibility. Then his left. Then his massive head moved from side to side. At last he thumped his tail against the far rocks of the cave. It was a signal the little dragons loved.

Sskarma was first to shout it out. "The story! He is going to tell us the story!" She ran quickly to her grandfather and curled around his front leg, sticking her tail into her mouth. The others took up their own special positions and waited for him to begin.

"And what good was this gift of sound?" asked the old dragon at last, picking up the tale as if a night and half a day had not come between tellings.

"What good?" asked the little dragons. Sskar muttered, "What good indeed?" over and over until Sskitter hit him on the tip of the nose with a claw.

This gift of sound *said Grandfather Dragon* that made the creature king could be used in many ways. He could coax the birds and beasts into his nets by making the sound of a hen calling the cock or a lioness seeking the lion or a bull elk spoiling for a fight. And so cock and lion and bull elk came. They came at this mighty hunter's calling, and they died at his hand.

Then the hunter learned the sounds that a dragon makes when he is hungry. He learned the sounds that a dragon makes when he is sleepy, when he looks for shelter, calls out warning, seeks a mate. All these great sounds of power the hunter learned—and more. And so one by one the lesser dragons came at his calling; one by one they came—and were killed.

The little dragons stirred uneasily at this. Sskarma shivered and put her tail into her mouth once more.

So we dragons named him *Ssgefah*, which, in the old tongue, means enemy. But he called himself Man.

"Man," they all said to one another. "Ssgefah. Man."

At last one day the Great-Grandfather of All Dragons looked around and saw that there were only two dragons left in the whole world—he and his mate. The two of them had been very cunning and had hidden themselves away in a mountain fastness, never answering any call but a special signal that they had planned between themselves.

"I know that signal," interrupted Sskitter. She gave a shuddering, hissing fall of sound.

The old dragon smiled at her, showing 147 of his secondary teeth. "You have learned it well, child. But do not use it in fun. It is the most powerful sound of all."

The little dragons all practiced the sound under their breaths while the old dragon stretched and rubbed an itchy place under his wing.

"Supper!" hissed Mother Dragon, landing on the stone outcropping by the cave mouth. She carried a mountain goat in her teeth. But the little dragons ignored her.

"Tell the rest," pleaded Sskarma.

"Not the rest," said the old dragon, "but I will tell you the next part."

3

"We must find a young Man who is unarmed," said the Great-Grandfather of All Dragons. "One who has neither net nor spear."

"And *eat* him!" said his mate. "It has been such a long time since we have had any red meat. Only such grasses and small birds as populate tops of mountains. It is dry, ribey fare at best." She yawned prettily and showed her sharp primary teeth.

"No," said the Great-Grandfather of All Dragons. "We shall capture him and learn his tongue. And then we will seal a bargain between us."

His mate looked shocked. Her wings arched up, great ribbed wings they were, too, with the skin between the ribbings as bright as blood. "A bargain? With such a puny thing as Man?"

The Great-Grandfather of All Dragons laughed sadly then. It was a dry, deep, sorrowful chuckle. "Puny?" he said, as quietly as smoke. "And what are we?"

"Great!" she replied, staring black eye into black eye. "Magnificent. Tremendous. Awe inspiring." She stood and stretched to her fullest, which was 450 slithes in length. The mountaintop trembled underneath her magnificently ponderous legs.

"You and I," said the Great-Grandfather of All Dragons, "and who else?"

She looked around, saw no other dragons, and was still.

"Why, that's just what you said last night, Grand-father," said little Sskitter.

Grandfather Dragon patted her on the head. "Good girl. Bright girl. Perceptive girl."

Sskar drew his claws lazily over the floor of the cave, making awful squeaks and leaving scratches in the stone. "I knew that," he said. Then he blew smoke rings to show he did not care that his sister had been praised.

But the other dragons were not afraid to show they cared. "I remember," said Ssgrum.

"Me, too," said Sstok.

They both came in for their share of praises.

Sskarma was quiet and stared. Then she said, "But more story, Grandfather."

"First comes supper," said Mother Dragon. "Growing bodies need to eat."

This time they all listened.

But when there was not even a smidgeon of meat left, and only the bones to gnaw and crack, Mother Dragon relented.

"Go ahead now," she said. "Tell them a story. But no nonsense."

"This is True History," said Sskitter.

"It's dumb!" said Sskar. He roared his roar again.

"How could there be us if they were the last of the dragons?"

"It's a story," said Sskarma. "And a story should be its own reward. I want to hear the rest."

The others agreed. They settled down again around Grandfather Dragon's legs, except for Sskar, who put his back against the old dragon's tail. That way he could listen to the story but pretend not to be interested.

4

So the Great-Grandfather of All Dragons *began the story once more* flew that very night on silent wings, setting them so that he could glide and catch the currents of air. And he was careful not to roar or to breathe fire or to singe a single tree.

He quartered town after town, village after village, farm after farm all fitted together as carefully as puzzles. And at last he came to a young shepherd boy asleep beside his flock out in a lonely field.

The Great-Grandfather of All Dragons dropped silently down at the edge of the field, holding his smoke so that the sheep—silly creatures—would not catch the scent of him. For dragons, as you know, have no odor other than the brimstone smell of their breath. The black-and-white sheepdog with the long hair twitched once, as if the sound of the Great-Grandfather's alighting had jarred his sleep, but he did not awaken.

Then the Great-Grandfather of All Dragons crept forward slowly, trying to sort out the sight and sound and smell of the youngling. He seemed to be about twelve Man years old and unarmed except for his shepherd's staff. He was fair haired and had a sprinkling of spots over the bridge of his nose that Men call freckles. He wore no shoes and smelled of cheese and bread, slightly moldy. There was also a green smell coming from his clothes, a tree and grass and rain and sun smell, which the Great-Grandfather of All Dragons liked.

The boy slept a very deep sleep. He slept so deeply because he thought that the world was rid of dragons, that all he had to worry about were wolves and bears and the sharp knife of hunger. Yes, he believed that dragons were no more until he dreamed them and screamed—and woke up, still screaming, in a dragon's claw.

Sskar applauded. "I like the part about the dragon's claw," he said, looking down at his own golden nails.

Sskitter poked him with her tail, and he lashed back. They rolled over and over until the old dragon separated them with his own great claws. They settled down to listen.

But when he saw that screaming would not help, the young Man stopped screaming, for he was very brave for all that he was very young.

And when he was set down in the lair and saw he

could not run off because the dragon's mate had blocked the door, the young Man made a sign against his body with his hand and said, "Be gone, Worm." For that is how Man speaks.

"Be gone, Worm," Sskitter whispered under her breath.

And Sskarma made the Man sign against her own body, head to heart, shoulder to shoulder. It did not make sense to her, but she tried it anyway.

Sskar managed to look amused, and the two younger dragons shuddered.

"Be gone, Worm," the Manling said again. Then he sat down on his haunches and cried, for he was a very young Man after all. And the sound of his weeping was not unlike the sound of a baby dragon calling for its food.

At that, the Great-Grandmother of All Dragons moved away from the cave mouth and curled herself around the Man and tried to comfort him, for she had no hatchlings of her own yet, though she had wished many years for them. But the Man buffeted her with his fist on the tender part of her nose, and she cried out in surprise—and in pain. Her roar filled the cave. Even the Great-Grandfather closed his earflaps. And the young Man held his hands up over the sides of his face and screamed back. It was not a good beginning.

But at last they both quieted down, and the Manling

stretched out his hand toward the tender spot and touched it lightly. And the Great-Grandmother of All Dragons opened her second eyelid—another surprise—and the great fires within her eyes flickered.

It was then that the Great-Grandfather of All Dragons said quietly in dragon words, "Let us begin."

The wonder of it was that the young Man understood.

"My name," he replied in Man talk, in a loud, sensible voice, "is Georgi." He pointed to himself and said "Georgi" again.

The Great-Grandfather of All Dragons tried. He said "Ssgggi," which we have to admit was not even close.

The Great-Grandmother of All Dragons did not even try.

So the youngling stood and walked over, being careful not to make any sudden gestures, and pointed straight at Great-Grandfather's neck.

"Sskraken," roared Great-Grandfather, for as you know a dragon always roars out his own name.

"Sskar!" roared Sskar, shattering a nearby tree. A small, above-the-frost-line tree. The others were silent, caught up in the story's spell.

And when the echo had died away, the youngling said in a voice as soft as the down on the underwing of an owl, "Sskraken." He did not need to shout it to be heard, but every syllable was there. It made the Great-Grandfather shiver. It made the Great-Grandmother put her head on the floor and think.

"Sskraken," the youngling said again, nodding as if telling himself to remember. Then he turned to Sskraken's mate and pointed at her. And the pointing finger never trembled.

"Sskrema," she said, as gently as a lullaby. It was the first time in her life that she had not roared out her name.

The youngling walked over to her, rubbed the spot on her nose that had lately been made sore. "Sskrema," he crooned. And to both their astonishments, she thrummed under his hand.

"She thrummed!" said Sskitter. "But you have told us . . ."

"Never to thrumm except to show the greatest happiness with your closest companions," the youngest two recited dutifully.

"So I did," said Grandfather Dragon. With the tip of his tail, he brushed away a fire-red tear that was caught in his eye. But he did it cleverly, so cleverly the little dragons did not notice. "So I did."

"Fah!" said Sskar. "It was a mistake. All a mistake. She never would have thrummed knowingly at a Man."

"That's what makes it so important," answered Sskarma. She reached up with her tail and flicked another tear from the old dragon's eye, but so cleverly

the others never noticed. Then she thrummed at him.
"Tell us more."

5

The youngling Georgi lived with the two saurs for a
year and a day. He learned many words in the old
tongue: "sstek" for red meat and "sstik" for the dry,
white meat of birds; "ssova," which means egg, and
"ssouva," which means soul. Learning the old tongue
was his pleasure, his task, and his gift.

In return, the Great-Grandfather of All Dragons and
his mate learned but one word. It was the name of the
Man—Georgi. Or as they said it, "Ssgggi."

At the end of the year and a day, the Great-
Grandfather called the boy to him, and they walked
away from the sweet-smelling nest of grasses and pine
needles and attar of wild rose that Georgi had built
for them. They walked to the edge of the jagged mountainside where they could look down on the rough waste
below.

"Ssgggi," said the Great-Grandfather of All Dragons
speaking the one word of Man's tongue he had learned,
though he had never learned it right. "It is time for
you to go home. For though you have learned much
about us and much from us you are not a dragon but
a Man. Now you must take your learning to them, the
Men, and talk to them in your own Man's tongue. Give
them a message from us. A message of peace. For if
you fail, we who are but two will be none." And he

gave a message to the Man.

Georgi nodded and then quietly walked back to the cave. At his footsteps, the Great-Grandmother of All Dragons appeared. She looked out and stared at the boy. They regarded one another solemnly, without speaking. In her dark eyes the candle flame flickered.

"I swear that I will not let that light go out," said Georgi, and he rubbed her nose. And then they all three thrummed at one another, though the Man did it badly.

Then he turned from the saurs without a further good-bye. And this was something else he had learned from the Great-Grandfather, for Men tend to prolong their good-byes, saying meaningless things instead of leaping swiftly into the air.

"It is their lack of wings," said Sskarma thoughtfully.

Georgi started down the mountain, the wind in his face and a great roar at his back. The mountains shook at his leaving, and great boulders shrugged down the cliff sides. And high above him, the two saurs circled endlessly in the sky, guarding him though he knew it not.

And so the Manling went home and the dragons waited.

"Dragons have a long patience," the two youngest saurs recited dutifully. "That is their genius." And

*when no one applauded their memories, they clattered
their own claws together and smiled at one another,
toothy smiles, and slapped their tails on the stone floor.*

6

In Dragon years *continued Grandfather Dragon* it was
but an eyelid's flicker, though in Man years it was a
good long while.

And then one day, when the bright eye of the sun
was for a moment shuttered by the moon's dark lid, a
great army of Men appeared at the mouth of the can-
yon and rode their horses almost to the foot of the
mountain.

The Great-Grandmother of All Dragons let her rough
tongue lick around her jaws at the sight of so much
red meat.

"Sstek," she said thoughtfully.

But the Great-Grandfather cautioned her, remembering how many dragons had died in fights with Men,
remembering the message he had sent with the Manling. "We wait," he said.

*"I would not have waited," hissed Sskar, lashing
his tail.*

*His sister Sskitter buffeted him on the nose. He cried
out once, and was still.*

At the head of the Men was one man in white armor
with a red figure emblazoned on his white shield.

It was when he saw this that Great-Grandfather sighed. "Ssgggi," he said.

"How can you tell?" asked the Great-Grandmother. "He is too big and too wide and too old for our Ssgggi. Our Ssgggi was this tall," and she drew a line into the pine tree that stood by the cave door.

"Men do not grow as dragons grow," reminded the Great-Grandfather gently. "They have no egg to protect their early days. Their skin is soft. They die young."

The Great-Grandmother put her paw on a certain spot on her nose and sighed. "It is not *our* Ssgggi," she said again. "He would not lead so many Men to our cave. He would not have to wear false scales on his body. He would come to the mountain by himself. I am going to scorch that counterfeit Ssgggi. I will roast him before his friends and crack his bones and suck out the marrow."

Then Great-Grandfather of All Dragons knew that she spoke out of sorrow and anger and fear. He flicked a red tear from his own eye with his tail and held it to her. "See, my eyes cry for our grown-up and grown-away Manling," he said. "But though he is bigger and older, he is our Ssgggi nonetheless. I told him to identify himself when he returned so that we might know him. He has done so. What do you see on his shield?"

The Great-Grandmother rose to her feet and peered closely at the Man so many slithes below them. And those dragon eyes which can see even the movement

of a rabbit cowering in its burrow, saw the red dragon
crouched on the white shield.

*"I can see a mole in its den," said Sskar. "I can see
a shrew in its tunnel. I can see . . ."*

*"You will see very little when I get finished with you
if you do not shut up," said Sskitter and hit him once
again.*

"I see a red dragon," said the Great-Grandmother,
her tail switching back and forth with anger.

"And what is the dragon doing?" asked the Great-
Grandfather even more gently.

She looked again. Then she smiled, showing every
one of her primary teeth. "It is covering a certain spot
on its nose," she said.

7

Just then the army stopped at a signal from the white
knight. They dismounted from their horses and waited.
The white knight raised his shield toward the mountain
and shouted. It took a little while for his voice to reach
the dragons, but when it did, they both smiled, for the
white knight greeted them in the old tongue.

He said: "I send greetings. I am Ssgggi, the dragon
who looks like a Man. I am taller now, but nowhere
near as tall as a dragon. I am wiser now, but nowhere near as wise as a dragon. And I have brought
a message from Men."

"Of course they did not trust him. Not a Man," hissed Sskar.

"They trusted this Man," said Sskitter. "Oh I know they did. I know I do."

Sskarma closed her eyes in thought. The other two little dragons were half asleep.

Grandfather Dragon did not answer their questions, but let the story answer the questions for him.

The Great-Grandfather of All Dragons stretched and rose. He unfurled his wings to their farthest point and opened his mouth and roared out gout after gout of flames. All the knights save the white knight knelt in fear then. And then Great-Grandfather pumped his wings twice and leaped into the air. Boulders buffeted by the winds rolled down the mountainside toward the Men.

The Great-Grandmother followed him, roaring as she flew. And they circled around and around in a great, widening gyre that was much too high for the puny Man arrows to reach.

Then the white knight called on all his archers to put down their bows, and the others to put aside their weapons. Reluctantly they obeyed, though a few grumbled angrily and they were all secretly very much afraid.

When the white knight saw that all his knights had disarmed themselves, the white knight held his shield up once more and called out "Come, Worm" in his own

{}

tongue. He made the Man sign again, head to heart, shoulder to shoulder. At that signal, the Great-Grandfather of All Dragons and his mate came down. They crested a current of air and rode it down to the knight's feet.

When they landed, they jarred nearly fifty slithes of earth, causing several of the Men to fall over in amazement or fear or from the small quaking of the ground. Then they lowered their heads to Ssgggi.

And the Man walked over to them, and first to the Great-Grandmother and then to the Great-Grandfather he lifted his fist and placed it ever so gently on a certain spot on the nose.

The Great-Grandmother thrummed at this. And then the Great-Grandfather thrummed as well. And the white knight joined them. The two dragons' bodies shook loud and long with their thrumming. And the army of Men stared and then laughed and finally cheered, for they thought that the Great-Grandparents were afraid.

"Afraid? Afraid of puny Men? They were shaking because they were thrumming. Only lower animals like rabbits and lion and deer—and Men—shake when they are afraid. I'll show them afraid!" cried Sskar. He leaped into the air and roared so hard that this time real flames came out of his nose slits, which so surprised him that he turned a flip in the air and came back to earth on his tailbone, which hurt enormously.

Grandfather Dragon ignored him, and so did the other little dragons. Only Mother Dragon, from her corner in the cave, chuckled. It was a sound that broke boulders.

Sskar limped back proudly to his grandfather's side, eager to hear the rest of the story. "I showed them, didn't I?" he said.

8

"Hear this," said the white knight Georgi, first in Man talk and then in the old tongue so that the dragons could understand as well. "From now on dragons shall raid no Man lands, and Men shall leave dragons alone. We will not even recognize you should we see you. You are no longer real to us.

"In turn, dragons will remain here, in this vast mountain wilderness untouched by Men. You will not see us or prey on us. You will not even recognize us. We are no longer real to dragons."

Great-Grandfather roared out his agreement, as did Great-Grandmother. Their roaring shattered a small mountain, which, to this day, Men call Dragon Fall. Then they sprang up and were gone out of the sight of the army of Men, out of the lives of Men.

"Good," said Sskar. "I am glad they are out of our sight and out of our lives. Men are ugly and unappetizing. We are much better off without them." He stretched and curled and tried to fall asleep. Stories

made him feel uncomfortable and sleepy at the same time.

But Sskitter was not happy with the ending. "What of Ssgggi?" she said. "Did they ever see him again? Of all Men, he was my favorite."

"And what of the Dragons' Thanksgiving?" said the littlest two, wide awake now.

Sskarma was silent, looking far out across the plains, across to Dragon's Fall, where the boulders lay all in a jumble.

Grandfather touched Sskarma's shoulder gently. "There is more," he said.

She turned her head to look at him, her black eyes glistening. "I know," she said. "Ssgggi came back. He would have to. He loved them so. And they loved him."

Grandfather shook his head. "No," he said. "He never came back. He could not. Dragons no longer existed for him, except in his heart. Did not exist for him—or for any Men. Of course," Grandfather added, "Men still exist for us. We do not have Man's gift of tongue or of the imagination. What is—for dragons—is. We cannot wish it away. We cannot make the real unreal, or the unreal real. I envy Man this other gift."

Sskarma closed her eyes and tried not to cry. "Never?" she said softly. "He never came back? Then how could there have been a Thanksgiving?"

Dragons keep promises *Grandfather continued,* for they do not have the imagination to lie. And so Great-

Grandfather and Great-Grandmother and all their children, for they finally had many, and their children's
children never bothered Men again. And, since Men
did not believe Dragons existed, Men did not bother
Dragons. That is what dragons give thanks for. In fact,
Men believed that Saint George—as they called him
in later years—had rid them forever of Dragons.

And so things have stood to this very day.

9

*Mother Dragon rose at the story's end. "You have a
Man's imagination, old one, though you deny it. You
have a gift for making up stories, which is another
way of saying you lie. Sometimes I think you are more
Man than dragon."*

*"I tell the truth," growled the old dragon. "This is
dragon history." Huffily, he cleaned his front claws.*

*"It is true that the word history contains the word
story," said Mother Dragon. "But that is the only thing
I will admit."*

*Grandfather Dragon houghed, and the smoke strag-
gled out of his nose slits.*

*"And now if we are to have a real old-fashioned
Dragon Thanksgiving, to celebrate the end of stories
and the beginning of food, I will have to go hunting
again," said Mother Dragon. "A deer I think. I saw
a fat herd by Dragon's Fall, grazing on the sweet spring
grass."*

"May I come?" asked Sskar.

*Mother Dragon smiled and groomed his tail for him.
"Now that you have real flames you may."*

*"The others and I will gather chestnuts," said
Grandfather. "For the celebration. For Thanksgiving."*

*Sskarma shook her head. "I would like to stay be-
hind and clean the cave."*

*The others left without an argument. No one liked
to clean the cave, sweeping the bones over the side of
the cliff. Mother Dragon and Sskar rose into the air,
banked to the left, and winged out of sight so that they
could approach the Fall from downwind. Grandfather
Dragon and the three young dragons moved slowly
along the deeply rutted mountain path.*

*Sskarma waited until they had all left; then she went
out and looked at the great old pine tree that grew near
the cave mouth. About five slithes up was a slash of
white, the mark left by a dragon nail, a slash they all
called* Ssgggi's *mark. She looked at it for a long time
and calculated how quickly trees grow. Then she stood
up alongside the tree. The mark came up to her shoulder.*

*"Ssgggi," she said. Then she said it three more times.
The fourth time she said it, it came out "Georgi."*

*"Georgi," she said a fifth time. This time it sounded
right. Smiling quietly to herself, Sskarma glanced
around the wilderness and then once into the sky. Far
away she could see one of the great silver birds Grandfather always warned them about. "Georgi," she said,
and went back in to clean the cave.*

7
Laughter in the Leaves

by Charles de Lint

> *. . . but the wind was always*
> *laughter in the leaves to me.*
> —*Wendelessen, from*
> *An Fear Glas*

"Listen," Meran said.

By the hearth, her husband laid his hands across the strings of his harp to still them and cocked his head. "I don't hear a thing," he said. "Just the wind."

"That's just it," Meran replied. "It's on the wind. Laughter. Giggles. I tell you, he's out there again."

Cerin laid his instrument aside. "I'll go see," he said.

Outside, the long gray skies of autumn were draining into night. The wind that came down from the heaths was gusting through the forest, rattling the leaves, gathering them up in eddying whirls and rushing them between the trees in a swirling dance. The moon was just starting to tip the eastern horizon, but there was no one out there. Only Old Badger, lying in his special spot between the cottage and the rosebushes, who lifted his striped head and made a questioning sort of noise at the harper standing in the doorway.

"Did you see him?" Cerin asked.

The badger regarded him for a few moments, then laid his head back down on his crossed forepaws.

"I've only seen him once myself," Meran said, joining Cerin at the door. "But I know he's out there. He knows you're going tomorrow and is letting me know that he means to play a trick or two while you're gone."

"Then I won't go."

"Don't be silly. You have to go. You promised."

"Then you must come. You were invited."

"I think I'd prefer putting up with our bodach's tricks to listening to the dry talk of harpers for two whole nights—and the day in between too, I'll wager."

Cerin sighed. "It won't be all talk. . . ."

"Oh, no," Meran replied with a smile. "There'll be fifteen versions of the same tune, all played in a row, and then a discussion as to which of twenty titles is the oldest for this particular tune. Wonderfully interesting stuff, I don't doubt, but it's not for me. And besides," she added after stooping down to give Old

Badger a quick pat and then closing the door, "I mean to have a trick or two ready for our little bodach myself this time."

Cerin sighed again. He believed there was a bodach, even though neither he nor anyone but Meran had ever seen it (and even then only in passing from the corner of her eye), but sometimes he had to wonder if every bit of mischief that took place around the cottage could be blamed on it. Whether it was a broken mug or a misplaced needle, it was always the bodach this and the bodach that.

"I don't know if it's such a wise idea to go playing tricks on a bodach," he said as he made his way back to the hearth. "They're quick to anger and—"

"So am I!" Meran interrupted. "No, Cerin. You go to your Harpers' Meet and don't worry about me. One way or another, we'll have come to an agreement while you're gone. Now play me a tune before we go to bed. He's gone now—I can tell. Do you hear the wind?"

Cerin nodded. But it sounded no different to him now than it had before.

"The smile's gone from it," Meran explained. "That's how you can tell that he's gone."

"I don't know why you don't just let me catch him with a harpspell."

Meran shook her head. "Oh, no. I'll best this little fellow with my wits, or not at all. I made that bargain with myself the first time he tripped me in the woods. Now come. Where's that tune you promised me?"

Cerin brought Telynros up onto his lap, and soon the cottage rang with the music that spilled from the roseharp's strings. Outside, Old Badger listened, and the wind continued to make a dance of the leaves among the trees, and only Meran could have said if the smile returned to its voice or not, but she would speak no more of bodachs that night.

The morning Cerin left, Meran's favorite mug fell from the shelf where it was perched and shattered on the stone floor; her hair when she woke was a tangle of elfknots that she didn't even bother to comb out; and the porridge boiled over for all that she stood over it and stirred and watched and took the best of care. She stamped her foot, but neither she nor Cerin made any comment. She saw him to the road with a smile, gave him a kiss and a jaunty wave along his way, and watched him go. Not until he was lost from sight, up the track and over the hill, with the sun in his eyes and the wind at his back, did she turn and face the woods, arms akimbo, to give the trees a long considering look.

"Now we'll see," she said.

She returned to the cottage, Old Badger at her heels.

The morning passed with her pretending to ignore the presence she knew was watching her from the forest. She combed out her hair, unraveling each knot that the little gnarled fingers of an elfman had tied in it last night. She picked up the shards of her mug, cleaned the burnt porridge from the stove, then straightened the kindling pile that had toppled over with a clatter and spill while she was busy inside the cottage. The smile on her lips was a little thin, but it never faltered.

She hummed to herself and it seemed that the wind in the trees put words to the tune:

> *Catch me, snatch me,*
> *catch me if you can!*
> *You'll never put the fetters*
> *on a little kowrie man!*

"That's as may be," Meran said as she got the last of the kindling stacked once more. She tied it in place with knots that only an Oakmaid would know, for she was the daughter of the Oak King of Ogwen Wood and knew a spell or two of her own. "But we'll still see."

When she went back inside, she could hear the kindling sticks rattle about a bit, but her knots held firm. And so it went through the day. She rearranged everything in the cottage, laying tiny holding spells here, there, and everywhere. She hung fetishes over each window—tiny bundles made up of dried oak leaves and acorns to represent herself, wren's feathers for Cerin, a lock of bristly badger hair for Old Badger, and rowan sprigs for their magic to seal the spell. Only the door she left untouched. By then twilight was at hand, stealing soft-footed across the wood, so she pulled up a chair to face the door and sat down to wait.

And the night went by.

The wind made teasing sounds around the cottage; Old Badger slept under her chair. She stayed awake, watching the door, firmly resolved to stay up the whole night if that was what it took. But as the hours crept by after midnight, she nodded, blinked awake, nodded again, and finally slept. When she woke in the morning, the door stood ajar, her hair was a crow's nest of tangles, and there was a small mocking stick figure drawn with charcoal on the floor at her feet, one arm lifted and a wide grin almost making two halves of the head.

The wind gusted through the door as soon as she was awake, sending a great spill of leaves that rattled like laughter across the floor. Stiff from an uncomfortable night spent in a chair, Meran made herself some tea and went outside to sit on the stoop. She refused to show even a tad of the frustration she felt. Instead she calmly drank her tea, pulled loose the new night's worth of tangles, then went inside to sweep the leaves and other debris from the cottage. The stick figure she left where it had been drawn to remind her of last night's failure.

"Well," she said to Old Badger as she went to set down a bowl of food for him. "And what did you see?"

The striped head lifted, eyes mournful, until the bowl was on the floor. And then he was too busy to reply—even if he'd had a voice with which to do so.

Meran knew she should get some rest for the next night, but she was too busy trying to think up a new way to stay awake to be able to sleep. It was self-contradictory, and she knew it, but it couldn't be helped. A half year of the bodach's tricks was too long. Five minutes' worth would be too long. As it drew near the supper hour, she finally gave up trying to rest and went to the well for water. A footfall on the road startled her as she was drawing the bucket up. She turned, losing her grip on the well's rope. The bucket went rattling down the well until it hit the bottom with a heavy splash. But she didn't hear it. Her attention was on the figure that stood on the track.

It was an old man that was standing there, an old traveling man in a tattered blue coat and yellow breeches, with his tinker's pack on his back and his face brown as a nut and lined with age. He regarded her with a smile, blue eyes twinkling.

"Evening, ma'am," he said. "It's been an awfully dry road I've been wending, no doubt about that. Could you see yourself clear to sparing me a drink from that well of yours?"

It's the bodach, Meran thought. Oh, you mischief maker, I have you now.

"Of course," she replied, smiling sweetly. "And you'll stay for supper, won't you?"

"Oh, no, ma'am. I wouldn't want to put you to any trouble."

"It's no trouble at all."

"That's kind of you."

Meran drew the bucket up once more. "Come along to the house and we'll brew up some tea—it'll do more for your thirst than just water."

"Oh, it does that," the old man agreed as he followed her back to the cottage.

Meran watched him with many a sidelong glance as they entered the cottage. He gave the chair facing the door an odd look, and the charcoal drawing an even odder one, but said nothing. By playing the part of an old tinker man, she supposed, the bodach meant to stay in character. A tinker would know better than to make remarks about whatever oddities his hostess might have in her house. He laid his pack by the door, and Meran put the kettle on.

"Have you been traveling far?" she asked.

"Oh, far enough for these old bones. I'm bound for Matchtem—by the sea, you know. My son has a wagon there, and we winter a little farther down the coast near Applewater."

Meran nodded. "Do have a seat," she said.

The old man looked around. She was busy at the table where the other chair was, so he sat down gingerly in the one facing the door. No sooner was he sitting than Meran slipped up behind him and tossed a chain of tiny iron links over him, tying it quickly to the chair. Oh, the links were small, and a boy could have easily broken free of them, but anything with iron in it bound a bodach or one of the kowrie folk. Everyone knew that. Meran danced around in front of the chair.

"Now I have you!" she cried. "Oh, you wicked bo-dach! I'll teach you to play your tricks on me."

"I *am* an old man," the tinker said, eyeing her carefully, "but I've played no tricks on you, ma'am—or at least none that I know of. My name's Yocky John, and I'm just a plain traveling man."

Meran smiled at the name, for she knew a word or two in the old tinker language. Clever John, the bodach might call himself, but he wasn't clever enough for her.

"Oh?" she asked. "You didn't tangle my hair, nor break my crockery, nor play a hundred other little mischiefs and tricks on me? And who was it, then?"

"Is it trouble with the little folk you're having?" Yocky John asked.

"Just one. You. And I have you now."

"But you don't. All you've caught is an old tinker, too tired to even get up out of this chair now that he's sitting. But I can help you with your bodach, I surely can. Yocky John's got a trick or two for them."

Outside the wind made the leaves laugh as they rushed in a rattling spray against the walls of the cottage. Meran listened, then looked uncertainly at the tinker. Had she made a mistake, or was this just another of the bodach's mischiefs?

"What sort of tricks?" she asked.

"Well, first I must know how you've gained the little fellow's ill will."

"I don't know. There's no reason for it—save his nature."

"Oh, no," Yocky John said. "They always have a reason." He looked slowly around the room. "It's a snug place you have here—but it's not so old, is it?"

Meran shook her head. It was just a year now since she'd lost her tree—the tree that a wooderl needs to survive. It was only through Cerin and the spells of his roseharp that she was able to live without it and in this cottage that they'd built where her tree had once stood.

"A very snug place," the old man said. "Magicked, too, I'd say."

"My husband's a harper."

"Ah. That explains it. Harp magic's heady stuff. A bodach can't live in a harper's home—not without an invitation."

"Still he comes and goes as he pleases," Meran said. "He breaks things and disrupts things and generally causes no end of mischief. Who'd *want* to have a bodach living with them?"

"Well, it's cold in the winter," Yocky John said, "out in the woods, with no shelter but a cloak of leaves, maybe, or a rickety lean-to that the wind howls through. The winds of winter aren't a bodach's friends—not like the winds of summer are. And I know cold, too. Why do you think I winter with my son? Only a fool tries to sleep in the snow."

Meran sighed. She pictured a little kowrie man, huddled in a bare-limbed winter tree, shivering in the cold, denied the warmth of a cottage because of a harper's magics.

"Well, if he felt that way," she said, "why didn't he come to us? Surely he'd have seen that we never turn a guest away. Are we ogres?"

"Well, you know bodachs," Yocky John said. "He'd be too proud and too shy. They like to creep into a place, all secret like, and hide out in the rafters or wherever, paying for their way with the odd good turn or two. It's the winter that's hard on them—even magical kowrie folk like they are. The summer's not so bad, for then even an old man like myself can sleep out of doors. But in the winter . . ."

Meran sighed again. "I never thought of it like that," she said. She studied the tinker, a smile twinkling in her eyes. "Well. Yocky John the bodach. You're welcome to stay in our rafters through the winter—but mind you leave my husband and me some privacy. Do you hear? And no more tricks. Or this time I'll let his roseharp play a spell."

"I'm not a bodach," Yocky John said. "At least not as you mean it."

"Yes, I know. A bodach's an old man, too—or it was in the old days."

"Do I look like a kowrie man to you?"

Meran grinned. "Who knows what a kowrie man would look like? It all depends on the shape he chooses to wear when you see him, don't you think? And I see you sitting there with that wee bit of iron chain wrapped around you."

"That's only because I'm too tired to get up."

"Have it your way."

She removed the chain then and went back to making supper. When she called him to the table, Yocky John rose very slowly to his feet and made his way over to the table. Meran laughed, thinking, oh, yes, play the part to the hilt, you old trickster, and went and fetched his chair for him. They ate and talked awhile; then Meran went to bed, leaving the old man to sleep on the mound of blankets that she'd readied for him in front of the hearth. When she woke the next morning, he was gone. And so was the charcoal drawing on the floor.

"So," Cerin said when he came home that night. "How went the great war between the fierce mistress of the oak wood and the equally fierce bodach that challenged her?"

Meran looked up toward the rafters, where a small round face peered down at her for a moment, then quickly popped out of sight. It didn't look at all like the old tinker man she'd guested last night, but who could know what was what or who was who when it came to mischief makers like a bodach? And was a tinker all that different really? They were as much tricksters themselves. So whether Yocky John and the bodach were one and the same or merely similar, she supposed she'd never know.

"Oh, we made our peace," she said.

8

Carol Oneir's Hundredth Dream

by Diana Wynne Jones

Carol Oneir was the world's youngest best-selling dreamer. The newspapers called her the Infant Genius. Her photograph appeared regularly in all the daily papers and monthly magazines, showing Carol either sitting alone in an armchair looking soulful or nestling lovingly against her mama. Mama was very proud of Carol. So were Carol's publishers, Wizard Reverie Ltd. They marketed her product in big bright-blue genie jars tied with cherry-colored satin ribbon; but you could also buy the Carol Oneir Omnibus Pillow, bright pink and heart shaped, Carol's Dreamie Comics, the Carol Oneir Dream Hatband, the Carol Oneir Charm Bracelet, and a half a hundred other spin-offs.

Carol had discovered at the age of seven that she was one of those lucky people who can control what they dream about, and then loosen the dream in their minds so that a competent wizard can spin it off and bottle it for other people to enjoy. Carol loved dreaming. She had made no less than ninety-nine full-length dreams. She loved all the attention she got and all the expensive things her mama was able to buy for her. So it was a terrible blow to her when she lay down one night to start dreaming her hundredth dream and nothing happened at all.

It was a terrible blow to Mama too, who had just ordered a champagne breakfast to celebrate Carol's Dream Century. Wizard Reverie Ltd. were just as upset as Mama. Their nice Mr. Ploys got up in the middle of the night and came down to Surrey by the milk train. He soothed Mama, and he soothed Carol, and he persuaded Carol to lie down and try to dream again. But Carol still could not dream. She tried every day for the following week, but she had no dreams at all, not even the kind of dreams ordinary people have.

The only person who took it calmly was Dad. He went fishing as soon as the crisis started. Mr. Ploys and Mama took Carol to all the best doctors, in case Carol was overtired or ill. But she wasn't. So Mama took Carol up to Harley Street to consult Herman Mindelbaum, the famous mind wizard. But Mr. Mindelbaum could find nothing wrong either. He said Carol's mind was in perfect order and that her self-confidence was rather surprisingly high, considering.

In the car going home, Mama wept and Carol sobbed.

Mr. Ploys said frantically, "Whatever happens, we mustn't let a hint of this get to the newspapers!" But of course it was too late. Next day the papers all had headlines saying, CAROL ONEIR SEES MIND SPECIALIST and IS CAROL ALL DREAMED OUT? Mama burst into tears again, and Carol could not eat any breakfast.

Dad came home from fishing later that day to find reporters sitting in rows on the front steps. He prodded his way politely through them with his fishing rod, saying, "There is nothing to get excited about. My daughter is just very tired, and we're taking her to Switzerland for a rest." When he finally got indoors, he said, "We're in luck. I've managed to arrange for Carol to see an expert."

"Don't be silly, dear. We saw Mr. Mindelbaum yesterday," Mama sobbed.

"I know, dear. But I said an expert, not a specialist," said Dad. "You see, I used to be at school with Chrestomanci—once, long ago, when we were both younger than Carol. In fact, he lost his first life because I hit him round the head with a cricket bat. Now, of course, being a nine-lived enchanter, he's a great deal more important than Carol is, and I had a lot of trouble getting hold of him. I was afraid he wouldn't want to remember me, but he did. He said he'd see Carol. The snag is, he's on holiday in the South of France and he doesn't want the resort filling with newspapermen—"

"I'll see to all that," Mr. Ploys cried joyfully. "Chrestomanci! Mr. Oneir, I'm awed. I'm struck dumb!"

Two days later, Carol and her parents and Mr. Ploys boarded first-class sleepers in Calais on the Swiss Orient Express. The reporters boarded it too, in second-class sleepers and third-class seats, and they were joined by French and German reporters standing in the corridors. The crowded train rattled away through France until, in the middle of the night, it came to Strasbourg, where a lot of shunting always went on. Carol's sleeper, with Carol and her parents asleep in it, was shunted off and hitched to the back of the Riviera Golden Arrow, and the Swiss Orient went on to Zurich without her. Mr. Ploys went to Switzerland with it. He told Carol that, although he was really a dream wizard, he had skill enough to keep the reporters thinking Carol was still on the train. "If Chrestomanci wants to be private," he said, "it could cost me my job if I let one of these near him."

By the time the reporters discovered the deception, Carol and her parents had arrived in the seaside resort of Teignes on the French Riviera. There Dad—not without one or two wistful looks at the casino—unpacked his rods and went fishing. Mama and Carol took a horse-drawn cab up the hill to the private villa where Chrestomanci was staying.

They dressed in their best for the appointment. Neither of them had met anyone before who was more important than Carol. Carol wore ruched blue satin the same color as her genie bottles, with no less than three hand-embroidered lace petticoats underneath it.

She had on matching button boots and a blue ribbon in her carefully curled hair, and she carried a blue satin parasol. She also wore her diamond heart pendant, her brooch that said CAROL in diamonds, her two sapphire bracelets, and all six of her gold bangles. Her blue satin bag had diamond clasps in the shape of two Cs. Mama was even more magnificent in a cherry-colored Paris gown, a pink hat, and all her emeralds.

They were shown up to a terrace by a rather plain lady who, as Mama whispered to Carol behind her fan, was really rather overdressed for a servant. Carol envied Mama her fan. There were so many stairs to the terrace that she was too hot to speak when they got there. She let Mama exclaim at the wonderful view. You could see the sea and the beach, and look into the streets of Teignes from here. As Mama said, the casino looked charming and the golf links so peaceful. On the other side, the villa had its own private swimming pool. This was full of splashing, screaming children, and, to Carol's mind, it rather spoiled the view.

Chrestomanci was sitting reading in a deck chair. He looked up and blinked a little as they came. Then he seemed to remember who they were and stood up with great politeness to shake hands. He was wearing a beautifully tailored natural-silk suit. Carol saw at a glance that it had cost at least as much as Mama's Paris gown. But her first thought on seeing Chrestomanci was, Oh my! He's twice as good-looking as Francis! She pushed that thought down quickly and trod it under. It belonged to the thoughts she never even told Mama. But it meant that she rather despised Chrestomanci for being quite so tall and for having hair so black and such flashing dark eyes. She knew he was going to be no more help than Mr. Mindelbaum, and Mr. Mindelbaum had reminded her of Melville.

Mama meanwhile was holding Chrestomanci's hand between both of hers and saying, "Oh, sir! This is *so* good of you to interrupt your holiday on our account! But when even Mr. Mindelbaum couldn't find out what's stopping her dreams—"

"Not at all," Chrestomanci said, wrestling for his hand. "To be frank, I was intrigued by a case even Mindelbaum couldn't fathom." He signaled to the serving lady who had brought them to the terrace. "Milly, do you think you could take Mrs. . . . er . . . O'Dear downstairs while I talk to Carol?"

"There's no need for that, sir," Mama said, smiling. "I always go everywhere with my darling. Carol knows I'll sit quite quietly and not interrupt."

"No wonder Mindelbaum got nowhere," Chrestomanci murmured.

Then—Carol, who prided herself on being very observant, was never quite sure how it happened—Mama was suddenly not on the terrace anymore. Carol herself was sitting in a deck chair facing Chrestomanci in his deck chair, listening to Mama's voice floating up from below somewhere. "I never let Carol go anywhere alone. She's my own ewe lamb. . . ."

Chrestomanci leaned back comfortably and crossed his elegant legs. "Now," he said, "be kind enough to tell me exactly what you do when you make a dream."

This was something Carol had done hundreds of times by now. She smiled graciously and began, "I get a feeling in my head first, which means a dream is ready to happen. Dreams come when they will, you know, and there is no stopping them or putting them off. So I tell Mama, and we go up to my boudoir, where she helps me to get settled on the special couch Mr. Ploys had made for me. Then Mama sets the spin-off spool turning and tiptoes away, and I drop off to sleep to the sound of it gently humming and whirling. Then the dream takes me. . . ."

Chrestomanci did not take notes, as did Mr. Mindelbaum and the reporters. He did not nod at her encouragingly the way Mr. Mindelbaum had. He simply stared vaguely out to sea. Carol thought that the least he might do was to tell those children in the pool to keep quiet. The screaming and splashing were so loud that she almost had to shout. Carol thought he was being very inconsiderate, but she kept on.

"I have learned not to be frightened and to go where the dream takes me. It is like a voyage of discovery—"

"When is this?" Chrestomanci interrupted in an offhand sort of way. "Does this dreaming happen at night?"

"It can happen at any time," said Carol. "If a dream

is ready, I can go to my couch and sleep during the day."

"How very useful," murmured Chrestomanci. "So you can put up your hand in a dull lesson and say, 'Please can I be excused to go and dream?' Do they let you go home?"

"I ought to have explained," Carol said, keeping her dignity with an effort, "that Mama arranges lessons for me at home so that I can dream any time I need to. It's like a voyage of discovery, sometimes in caves underground, sometimes in palaces in the clouds—"

"Yes. And how long do you dream for? Six hours? Ten minutes?" Chrestomanci interrupted again.

"About half an hour," said Carol. "Sometimes in the clouds, or maybe in the southern seas. I never know where I will go or whom I will meet on my journey—"

"Do you finish a whole dream in half an hour?" Chrestomanci interrupted yet again.

"Of course not. Some of my dreams last for more than three hours," Carol said. "As for the people I meet, they are strange and wonderful—"

"So you dream in half-hour stretches," said Chrestomanci. "And I suppose you have to take a dream up again exactly where you left it at the end of the half hour before."

"Obviously," said Carol. "People must have told you— I can *control* my dreams. And I do my best work in regular half-hour stints. I wish you wouldn't keep interrupting, when I'm doing my best to tell you!"

Chrestomanci turned his face from the sea and looked at her. He seemed surprised. "My dear young lady, you are *not* doing your best to tell me. I do read the papers, you know. You are giving me precisely the same flannel you gave the *Times* and *Croydon Gazette* and the *People's Monthly*, and doubtless poor Mindelbaum as well. You are telling me your dreams come unbidden—but you have one for half an hour every day—and that you never know where you'll go in them or what will happen—but you can control your dreams perfectly. That can't all be true, can it?"

Carol slid the bangles up and down her arm and tried to keep her temper. It was difficult to do when the sun was so hot and the noise coming from that pool so loud. She thought seriously of demoting Melville and making Chrestomanci into the villain in her next dream—until she remembered that there might not *be* a next dream unless Chrestomanci helped her. "I don't understand," she said.

"Let's talk about the dreams themselves then," said Chrestomanci. He pointed down the terrace steps to the blue, blue water of the pool. "There you see my ward, Janet. She's the fair-haired girl the others are just pushing off the diving board. She loves your dreams. She has all ninety-nine of them—though I am afraid Julia and the boys are very contemptuous about it.

They say your dreams are slush and all exactly the same."

Naturally Carol was deeply hurt that anyone could call her dreams slush, but she knew better than to say so. She smiled graciously down at the large splash which was all she could see of Janet.

"Janet is hoping to meet you later," said Chrestomanci. Carol's smile broadened. She loved meeting admirers. "When I heard you were coming," Chrestomanci said, "I borrowed Janet's latest Omnibus Pillow." Carol's smile narrowed a bit. Chrestomanci did not seem the kind of person who would enjoy her dreams at all. "I enjoyed it rather," Chrestomanci confessed. Carol's smile widened. Well! "But Julia and the boys are right, you know," Chrestomanci went on. "Your happy endings are pretty slushy, and the same sort of things happen in all of them." Carol's smile narrowed again distinctly at this. "But they're terribly lively," Chrestomanci said. "There's so much action and so many people. I like all those crowds—what your blurbs call your 'cast of thousands,' but I must confess I don't find your settings very convincing. That Arabian setting in the ninety-sixth dream was awful, even making allowances for how young you are. On the other hand, your fairground in the latest dream seemed to show the makings of a real gift."

By this time, Carol's smile was going broad and narrow like the streets of Dublin's Fair City. She was almost caught off guard when Chrestomanci said, "And though you never appear in your dreams yourself, a number of characters do come in over and over again— in various disguises of course. I make it about five or six main actors in all."

This was getting far too close to the things Carol never told even Mama. Luckily some reporters had made the same observation. "This is the way dreams are," she said. "And I am only the Seeing Eye."

"As you told the *Manchester Guardian*," Chrestomanci agreed, "if that is what they meant by 'Oosung Oyo.' I see that must have been a misprint now." He was looking very vague, to Carol's relief, and did not seem to notice her dismay. "Now," he said, "I suggest the time has come for you to go to sleep and let me see what happened to send your hundredth dream so wrong that you refused to record it."

"But nothing went wrong!" Carol protested. "I just didn't dream."

"So you say," said Chrestomanci. "Close your eyes. Feel free to snore if you wish."

"But . . . but I can't just go to sleep in the middle of a visit!" Carol said. "And . . . and those children in the pool are making far too much noise."

Chrestomanci put one hand casually down to the paving of the terrace. Carol saw his arm go up as if he were pulling something up out of the stones. The terrace went quiet. She could see the children splashing below, and their mouths opening and shutting, but not a sound came to her ears. "Have you run out of excuses now?" he asked.

"They're not excuses. And how are you going to know whether I dream or not without a proper dream-spool and a qualified dream-wizard to read it?" Carol demanded.

"Oh, I daresay I can manage quite well without," Chrestomanci remarked. Though he said it in a mild, sleepy sort of way, Carol suddenly remembered that he was a nine-lived enchanter, and more important than she was. She supposed he thought he was powerful enough on his own. Well, let him. She would humor him. Carol arranged her blue parasol to keep some of the sun off her and settled back in her deck chair, knowing nothing was going to happen. . . .

. . . And she was at the fairground, where her ninety-ninth dream had left off. In front of her was a wide space of muddy grass, covered with bits of paper and other rubbish. She could see the Big Wheel in the distance behind some flapping tents and half-dismantled stalls, and another tall thing that seemed to be most of the Helter Skelter tower. The place seemed quite deserted.

"Well *really!*" Carol said. "They still haven't cleared anything up! What are Martha and Paul *thinking* of?"

As soon as she said that, she clapped her hands guiltily to her mouth and whirled round to make sure that Chrestomanci had not come stalking up behind her. But there was nothing behind her but more dreary,

litter-covered grass. Good! Carol thought. I *knew* nobody could come behind the scenes in a Carol Oneir
private dream unless I let them! She relaxed. She was
boss here. This was part of the things she never even
told Mama—though, for a moment, back on the terrace
at Teignes, she had been afraid that Chrestomanci was
onto her.

The fact was, as Chrestomanci had noticed, Carol
did only have six main characters working for her.
There was Francis, tall and fair and handsome, with
a beautiful baritone voice, who did all the heroes. He
always ended up marrying the gentle but spirited Lucy,
who was fair too and very pretty. Then there was
Melville, who was thin and dark, with an evil white
face, who did all the villains. Melville was so good at
being a Baddie that Carol often used him several times
in one dream. But he was always the gentleman, which
was why polite Mr. Mindelbaum had reminded Carol
of Melville. The other three were Bimbo, who was
oldish and who did all the Wise Old Men, Pathetic
Cripples, and Weak Tyrants; Martha, who was the
Older Woman and did the Aunts, Mothers, and Wicked
Queens, either straight wicked or with Hearts of Gold;
and Paul, who was small and boyish looking. Paul's
specialty was the Faithful Boy Assistant, though he
did Second Baddie too and tended to get killed quite
often in both kinds of parts. Paul and Martha, since
they never had very big parts, were supposed to see

that the cast of thousands cleared everything up between dreams.

Except that they hadn't this time.

"Paul!" Carol shouted. "Martha! Where's my cast of
thousands?"

Nothing happened. Her voice just went rolling away
into emptiness.

"Very well!" Carol called out. "I shall come and find
you, and you won't like it when I do!"

She set off, picking her way disgustedly through the
rubbish, toward those flapping tents. It really was too
bad of them, she thought, to let her down like this,
when she had gone to all the trouble of making them
up and giving them a hundred disguises, and had made
them as famous as she was herself, in a way. As Carol
thought this, her bare foot came down in a melted ice
cream. She jumped back with a shudder and found she
was, for some reason, wearing a bathing suit like the
children in Chrestomanci's pool.

"Oh really!" she said crossly. She remembered now
that her other attempt at a hundredth dream had gone
like this too, up to the point where she had scrapped
it. Anyone would think this was the kind of dream
ordinary people had. It wouldn't even make a decent
Hatband dream. This time, with a sternly controlled
effort, she made herself wear her blue button boots
and the blue dress with all its petticoats underneath.
It was hotter like that, but it showed that she was in

charge. And she marched on, until she came to the flapping tents.

Here it nearly came like a common dream again. Carol walked up and down among empty tents and collapsed stalls, under the great framework of the Big Wheel and repeatedly past the topless Helter Skelter tower, past roundabout after empty roundabout, without seeing a soul. It was only her stern annoyance that kept her going until she did see someone, and then she nearly went straight past him, thinking he was one of the dummies from the Waxworks Show. He was sitting on a box beside a painted organ from a roundabout, staring. Perhaps some of the cast of thousands did work as dummies when necessary, Carol thought. She had no idea really. But this one was fair, so that meant he was a Goodie and generally worked with Francis.

"Hey, you!" she said. "Where's Francis?"

He gave her a dull, unfinished sort of look. "Rhubarb," he said. "Abracadabra."

"Yes, but you're not doing a crowd scene now," Carol told him. "I want to know where my Main Characters are."

The man pointed vaguely beyond the Big Wheel. "In their quarters," he said. "Committee meeting." So Carol set off that way. She had barely gone two steps when the man called out from behind her. "Hey you! Say 'Thank you'!"

How rude! thought Carol. She turned and glared at him. He was now drinking out of a very strong-

smelling green bottle. "You're drunk!" she said. "Where
did you get that? I don't allow real drink in my dreams."

"Name's Norman," said the man. "Drowning sor-
rows."

Carol saw that she was not going to get any sense
out of him. So she said "Thank you," to stop him shouting after her again and went the way he had pointed.
It led her among a huddle of gypsy caravans. Since
these all had a blurred cardboard sort of look, Carol
went straight past them, knowing they must belong
to the cast of thousands. She knew the caravan she
wanted would look properly clear and real. And it did.
It was more like a tarry black shed on wheels than a
caravan, but there was real black smoke pouring out
of its rusty iron chimney.

Carol sniffed it. "Funny. It smells almost like toffee!" But she decided not to give her people any further
warning. She marched up the black wooden ladder to
the door and flung the door open.

Smoke and heat and the smell of drink and toffee
rolled out at her. Her people were all inside, but instead of turning politely to receive their orders as they
usually did, none of them at first took any notice of
her at all. Francis was sitting at the table playing cards
with Martha, Paul, and Bimbo by the light of candles
stuck in green bottles. Glasses of strong-smelling drink
stood at each of their elbows, but most of the drink
smell, to Carol's horror, was coming from the bottle
Lucy was drinking out of. Beautiful, gentle Lucy was

sitting on a bunk at the back, giggling and nursing a green bottle. As far as Carol could see in the poor light, Lucy's face looked like a gnome's and her hair was what Mama would describe as "in tetters." Melville was cooking at the stove near the door. Carol was ashamed to look at him. He was wearing a grubby white apron and smiling a dreamy smile as he stirred his saucepan. Anything less villainous was hard to imagine.

"And just what," said Carol, "do you think you're all doing?"

At that, Francis turned around enough for her to see that he had not shaved for days. "Shut that blesh door, can' you!" he said irritably. It was possible he spoke that way because he had a large cigar between his teeth, but Carol feared it was more likely to be because Francis was drunk.

She shut the door and stood in front of it with her arms folded. "I want an explanation," she said. "I'm waiting."

Paul slapped down his cards and briskly pulled a pile of money toward himself. Then he took the cigar out of his boyish mouth to say, "And you can go on waiting, unless you've come to negotiate at last. We're on strike."

"On strike!" said Carol.

"On strike," Paul said. "All of us. I brought the cast of thousands out straight after the last dream. We want better working conditions and a bigger slice of the cake." He gave Carol a challenging and not very

pleasant grin and put the cigar back in his mouth—a
mouth that was not so boyish, now Carol looked at it
closely. Paul was older than she had realized, with
little cynical lines all over his face.

"Paul's our shop steward," Martha said. Martha, to
Carol's surprise, was quite young, with reddish hair
and a sulky, righteous look. Her voice had a bit of a
whine to it when she went on. "We have our rights,
you know. The conditions the cast of thousands have
to live in are appalling, and it's one dream straight
after another and no free time at all for any of us. And
it's not as if we get job satisfaction, either. The rotten
parts Paul and I do!"

"Measly walk-ons," Paul said, busy dealing out cards.
"One of the things we're protesting is being killed almost every dream. The cast of thousands gets gunned
down in every final scene, and not only do they get no
compensation, they have to get straight up and fight
all through the next dream."

" 'nd never allowsh ush any dthrink," Bimbo put in.
Carol could see he was very drunk. His nose was pur-
ple with it, and his white hair looked damp. "Got shick
of colored water. Had to shteal fruit from Eshanted
Garden dream to make firsht wine. Make whishky now.
It'sh better."

"It's not as if you *paid* us anything," Martha whined.
"We have to take what reward we can get for our
services."

"Then where did you get all that money?" Carol

demanded, pointing to the large heap in front of Paul.

"The Arabian treasure scene and so forth," said Paul. "Pirates' hoard. Most of it's only painted paper."

Francis suddenly said, in a loud slurry voice, "I want recognition. I've been ninety-nine different heroes, but not a word of credit goes on any pillow or jar." He banged the table. "Exploitation! That's what it is!"

"Yes, we all want our names on the next dream," Paul said. "Melville, give her our list of complaints, will you?"

"Melville's our Strike Committee Secretary," said Martha.

Francis banged the table again and shouted, *"Melville!"* Then everyone else shouted, "MELVILLE!" until Melville finally turned round from the stove holding his saucepan in one hand and a sheet of paper in the other.

"I didn't want to spoil my fudge," Melville said apologetically. He handed the paper to Carol. "There, my dear. This wasn't my idea, but I didn't wish to let the others down."

Carol, by this time, was backed against the door, more or less in tears. This dream seemed to be a nightmare. "Lucy!" she called out desperately. "Lucy, are you in this too?"

"Don't you disturb her," said Martha, whom Carol was beginning to dislike very much. "Lucy's suffered enough. She's had her fill of parts that make her a

plaything and property of men. Haven't you, love?"
she called to Lucy.

Lucy looked up. "Nobody understands," she said,
staring mournfully at the wall. "I hate Francis. And
I always have to marry him and live hap-hic-hallipy
ever after."

This, not surprisingly, annoyed Francis. "And I hate
you!" he bawled, jumping up as he shouted. The table
went over with a crash, and the glasses, money, cards,
and candles went with it. In the terrifying dark scram-
ble that followed, the door somehow burst open behind
Carol, and she got herself out through it as fast as she
could . . .

. . . And found herself sitting on a deck chair on the
sunny terrace again. She was holding a paper in one
hand, and her parasol was rolling by her feet. To her
annoyance, someone had spilt a long, sticky trickle of
what seemed to be fudge all down her blue dress.

"Tonino! Vieni qui!" somebody called.

Carol looked up to find Chrestomanci trying to put
together a broken deck chair in the midst of a crowd
of people who were all pushing past him and hurrying
away down the terrace steps. Carol could not think
who the people were at first, until she caught a glimpse
of Francis among them, and then Lucy, who had one
hand clutched around her bottle and the other in the
hand of Norman, the man Carol had first met sitting
on a box. The rest of them must be the cast of thou-

sands, she supposed. She was still trying to imagine what had happened when Chrestomanci dropped the broken deck chair and stopped the very last person to cross the terrace.

"Excuse me, sir," Chrestomanci said. "Would you mind explaining a few things before you leave?"

It was Melville, still in his cook's apron, waving smoke away from his saucepan with one long, villainous hand and peering down at his fudge with a very doleful look on his long, villainous face. "I think it's spoiled," he said. "You want to know what happened? Well, I think the cast of thousands started it, around the time Lucy fell in love with Norman, so it may have been Norman's doing to begin with. Anyway, they began complaining that they never got a chance to be real people, and Paul heard them. Paul is very ambitious, you know, and he knew, as we all did, that Francis isn't really cut out to be a hero—"

"No indeed. He has a weak chin," Chrestomanci agreed.

Carol gasped and was just about to make a protest— which would have been a rather tearful one at that moment—when she recalled that Francis's bristly chin had indeed looked rather small and wobbly under that cigar.

"Oh you shouldn't judge by chins," said Melville. "Look at mine—and I'm no more a villain than Francis is a hero. But Francis has his petulant side, and Paul played on that, with the help of Bimbo and his whisky, and Lucy was with Paul anyway because she hated being forced to wear frilly dresses and simper at Francis. She and Norman want to take up farming. And Martha, who is a very frivolous girl to my mind, came in with them because she cannot abide having to clear up the scenery at such short notice. So then they all came to me."

"And you held out?" asked Chrestomanci.

"All through *The Cripple of Monte Christo* and *The Arabian Knight*," Melville admitted, ambling across the terrace to park his saucepan on the balustrade. "I am fond of Carol, you see, and I am quite ready to be three villains at once for her if that is what she wants. But when she started on the *Fairground* dream straight after *The Tyrant of London Town*, I had to admit that we were all being thoroughly overworked. None of us got any time to be ourselves. Dear me," he added. "I think the cast of thousands is preparing to paint the town red."

Chrestomanci came and leaned on the balustrade to see. "I fear so," he said. "What do you think makes Carol work you all so hard? Ambition?"

There was now such a noise coming from the town that Carol could not resist getting up to look too. Large numbers of the cast of thousands had made straight for the beach. They were joyously racing into the water, pulling little wheeled bathing huts after them, or simply casting their clothes away and plunging in. This was causing quite an outcry from the regular holidaymakers. More outcries came from the main square below the casino, where the cast of thousands had flooded into all the elegant cafés, shouting for ice-cream, wine, and frogs' legs.

"It looks rather fun," said Melville. "No, not ambition exactly, sir. Say rather that Carol was caught up in success, and her mama was caught up with her. It is not easy to stop something when one's mama expects one to go on and on."

A horse-drawn cab was now galloping along the main street, pursued by shouting, scrambling, excited people. Pursuing these was a little posse of gendarmes. This seemed to be because the white-bearded person in the cab was throwing handfuls of jewels in all directions in the most abandoned way. Arabian jewels and pirates' treasure mostly, Carol thought. She wondered if they would turn out to be glass or real jewels.

"Poor Bimbo," said Melville. "He sees himself as a sort of kingly Santa Claus these days. He has played those parts too often. I think he should retire."

"And what a pity your mama told your cab to wait," Chrestomanci said to Carol. "Isn't that Francis, Martha, and Paul, there? Just going into the casino."

They were, too. Carol saw them waltzing arm in arm up the marble steps, three people obviously going on a spree.

"Paul," said Melville, "tells me he has a system to break the bank."

"A fairly common delusion," said Chrestomanci.

"But he can't!" said Carol. "He hasn't got any real money!" She chanced to look down as she spoke. Her diamond pendant was gone. So was her diamond brooch. Her sapphire bangles and every one of her gold ones were missing. Even the clasps of her handbag had been torn off. "They robbed me!" she cried out.

"That would be Martha," Melville said sadly. "Remember she picked pockets in *The Tyrant of London Town*."

"It sounds as if you owed them quite a sum in wages," Chrestomanci said.

"But what shall I *do*?" Carol wailed. "How am I going to get everyone back?"

Melville looked worried for her. It came out as a villainous grimace, but Carol understood perfectly. Melville was sweet. Chrestomanci just looked surprised and a little bored. "You mean you *want* all these people back?" he said.

Carol opened her mouth to say yes, of course she did! But she did not say it. They were having such fun. Bimbo was having the time of his life galloping through the streets throwing jewels. The people in the sea were a happy splashing mass, and waiters were hurrying about down in the square, taking orders and slapping down plates and glasses in front of the cast of thousands in the cafés. Carol just hoped they were using real money. If she turned her head, she could see that some of the cast of thousands had now got as far as the golf course, where most of them seemed to be under the impression that golf was a team game that you played rather like hockey.

"While Carol makes up her mind," said Chrestomanci, "what, Melville, is your personal opinion of her dreams? As one who has an inside view?"

Melville pulled his mustache unhappily. "I was afraid you were going to ask me that," he said. "She has tremendous talent, of course, or she couldn't do it at all, but I do sometimes feel that she—well—she repeats herself. Put it like this: I think maybe Carol doesn't give herself a chance to be herself any more than she gives us."

Melville, Carol realized, was the only one of her people she really liked. She was heartily sick of all the others. Though she had not admitted it, they had bored her for years, but she had never had time to think of anyone more interesting, because she had always been so busy getting on with the next dream. Suppose she gave them all the sack? But wouldn't that hurt Melville's feelings?

"Melville," she said anxiously, "do you enjoy being villains?"

"My dear," said Melville, "it's up to you entirely, but I confess that sometimes I would like to try being someone . . . well . . . not black hearted. Say, *gray* hearted, and a little more complicated."

This was difficult. "If I did that," Carol said, thinking about it, "I'd have to stop dreaming for a while and spend a time—maybe a long time—sort of getting a new outlook on people. Would you mind waiting? It might take over a year."

"Not at all," said Melville. "Just call me when you need me." And he bent over and kissed Carol's hand, in his best and most villainous manner. . . .

. . . And Carol was once again sitting up in her deck chair. This time, however, she was rubbing her eyes, and the terrace was empty except for Chrestomanci, holding a broken deck chair, and talking in what seemed to be Italian to a skinny little boy. The boy seemed to have come up from the bathing pool. He was wearing bathing trunks and dripping water all over the paving.

"Oh!" said Carol. "So it was only a dream really!" She noticed she must have dropped her parasol while she was asleep and reached to pick it up. Someone seemed to have trodden on it. And there was a long trickle of fudge on her dress. Then of course she looked for her brooch, her pendant, and her bangles. They were gone. Someone had torn her dress pulling the brooch off. Her eyes leaped to the balustrade and found a small burnt saucepan standing on it.

At that, Carol jumped up and ran to the balustrade, hoping to see Melville on his way down the stairs from the terrace. The stairs were empty. But she was in time to see Bimbo's cab, surrounded by gendarmes and stopped at the end of the parade. Bimbo did not seem to be in it. It looked as if he had worked the disappearing act she had invented for him in *The Cripple of Monte Christo*. Down on the beach, crowds of the cast of thousands were coming out of the sea and lying down to sunbathe, or politely borrowing beach balls from the other holidaymakers. She could hardly tell them from the regular tourists, in fact. Out on the golf links, the cast of thousands there was being sorted out by a man in a red blazer, and lined up to practice tee shots. Carol looked at the casino then, but there was no sign of Paul or Martha or Francis. Around the square, however, there was singing coming from the crowded cafés—steady, swelling singing, for, of course, there were several massed choirs among the cast of thousands. Carol turned and looked accusingly at Chrestomanci.

Chrestomanci broke off his Italian conversation in order to bring the small boy over by one wet, skinny shoulder. "Tonino here," he said, "is a rather unusual magician. He reinforces other people's magic. When I saw the way your thoughts were going, I thought we'd better have him up to back up your decision. I suspected you might do something like this. That's why I didn't want any reporters. Wouldn't you like to come down to the pool now? I'm sure Janet can lend you a swimsuit and probably a clean dress as well."

"Well . . . thank you . . . yes, please . . . but . . ." Carol began, when the small boy pointed to something behind her.

"I speaka Eengleesh," he said. "You droppa youra paper."

Carol dived around and picked it up. In beautiful sloping writing, it said:

Carol Oneir hereby releases Francis, Lucy, Martha, Paul, and Bimbo from all further professional duties and gives the cast of thousands leave of indefinite absence. I am taking a holiday with your kind permission, and I remain

Your servant,

Melville.

"Oh good!" said Carol. "Oh dear! What shall I do about Mr. Ploys? And how shall I break it to Mama?"

"I can speak to Ploys," said Chrestomanci, "but your mama is strictly your problem, though your father, when he gets back from the casin—er, fishing—will certainly back you up."

Dad did back Carol up some hours later, and Mama was slightly easier to deal with than usual anyway, because she was so confused at the way she had mistaken Chrestomanci's wife for a servant. By that time, however, the main thing Carol wanted to tell Dad was that she had been pushed off the diving board sixteen times and had learned to swim two strokes—well, almost.

9
The Singing Float

by Monica Hughes

The singing woke Melissa, high, clear notes like those of a violin, at the very edge of hearing. She sat up in bed. The cabin was silent, the only light a strip of pure white between the not-quite-closed curtains across the window.

She slipped out of bed and padded to the window, her toes curling away from the chill of the floor. She pushed the drape aside and looked out. Beyond the fringe of pines the land dropped abruptly to the beach, and she could see, framed by the dark strokes of the trees, a line of silver stretching clear to the horizon.

It rippled like a bolt of silk flung down from the sky toward her feet. She stood, frozen in its magic, until the moon sailed out from behind an obscuring pine and the silken path became only its reflection on the still surface of the sea. She shivered, scampered back to bed, and lay in a ball, warming her feet with her hands, until she fell asleep.

When Melissa woke, the sun was shining in an ordinary sort of way. The tide was out and the memory of the singing and of the white moon's path was like a dream. She pulled on shorts and a T-shirt, made her bed neatly, and dusted her collection of shells with a tissue. That did not take long. She had collected only five, but each of them was perfect, without a flaw or a chip.

When everything was in order she ran into the living room, which was really living and dining room and kitchen all in one, with a fireplace where you could roast marshmallows and a big window overlooking the Pacific.

"Good morning, Half Pint."

"Morning, Daddy." She gave him a kiss and got her special hug in return. "Good morning, Mum. What's for breakfast?"

"Sausages and scrambled eggs. If you and Dad do the dishes."

"Worth it. I'm starving." She stood by the stove and carried the plates to the table as Mum filled them.

"Full moon last night. Extra high tide. Good pickings on the shore today, Lissa."

"Oh, I do hope so. Do you realize that we've only got two more days? Only *two*. I can't believe it."

"Me neither."

* * *

When breakfast was eaten and the dishes put away, Melissa picked her way carefully down the path to the beach. There were steps roughly carved between tree roots, and at the bottom was a tangle of weather-whitened timbers, painful to bare feet. She crossed it with care and then did what she did every morning: raced as fast as she could across the sand to the very edge of the sea.

Only then, standing with her toes dug into the wet sand, the sea foaming at her insteps, did she turn and look back along the beach. This was the magic moment. The moment of choice. Where shall I look today? Where is the best shell hiding? Above all, *will* there at last be a glass float?

Glass floats were as rare as hens' teeth, Daddy said, now that the Japanese fisherfolk had started using plastic floats of gaudy green and pink to hold up their gill nets and mark their traps, instead of the smoky iridescent globes of blown glass the size of a large grapefruit.

"Only two more days," she said as she stood with the water dragging at her toes. "Only *two* more days." She looked at the rocky headland to the north and along the white beach that curved around to the southern headland.

"Where, oh where, do I begin today?"

Into her mind came the high, clear note she had heard in the night. Slowly she followed the sound, walking over strands of shining brown kelp and pale half-buried logs and tree roots smoothed by the sea. She walked without thought toward a tangle of seaweed at the uppermost limit of last night's tide.

There, among fat cords and shiny ribbons and air bladders, was the faint glint of a rainbow. She dropped to her knees and gently loosened the strands one by one. There it was, perfect, like a huge frozen soap bubble. She lifted it out and cradled it in the palms of her hands. The singing in her head had stopped, and the whole morning was still.

"You beauty, oh you beauty," she whispered. For a brief second it seemed that something flickered in the depths of the glass globe. Then the sun dazzled on its curve and she blinked. When she looked again she could see nothing inside.

She got to her feet and began to walk slowly back toward their cabin, holding the float carefully in both hands.

"What have you got?" Mum turned as the screen door banged.

"Just look!"

"Oh, what a beauty."

"Clever girl."

Was I? she wondered. It had been more like being led than finding. She wadded some tissues in the center of the table and set the float down upon them. "Isn't it the most perfect thing in the whole world? I don't care if we have to go home in two days. I wouldn't care if we had to go tomorrow. Right now, even."

"Well, I would." Mum laughed. "I'm counting on two more days' fun with you and Dad. What's the plan, Phil, now Melissa has done her beachcombing?"

"I thought we might drive up to Tofino and take the boat out to look at the seals. Maybe even get a peek at a whale."

"Great idea. I've already packed lunch. Lissa, get your shoes and socks on. And better take a jacket. It might be cool on the water."

"But . . ." Melissa looked longingly at her float. Like a rainbow, she thought. Of my very own.

"Dear girl, you can't sit in here all day. The sun's shining. Go get your shoes, quick!"

"But . . ." she said as she went.

"*And* your jacket. Phil, have you got the thermos? And I've got the basket. Oh, Lissa, *do* wake up!"

Melissa followed them reluctantly out of the cabin. In the shadowy living room the globe glowed.

"Oh, I forgot to lock the door!" she cried out, halfway to Tofino. "Dad, we have to go back. My float . . ."

"It won't walk away. And I did check the door. My goodness, Lissa, I think you must be bewitched."

Perhaps I am, she thought, and kneeled on the backseat of the car, watching the road unwind between the pines, taking them farther and farther away from the cabin.

At any other time the boat ride to the seal rocks and beyond, almost out to the salmon fishing grounds, would have been the high point of the holidays. Indeed, part of Melissa enjoyed every moment. But the other part of her kept looking back to the low line of the shore and thinking: There is the bay. And there must be our cabin, and in it, on the table . . .

She gripped the aft railing so tightly that her knuckles went white. For one crazy minute she'd actually wanted to dive into the water and swim ashore, *she* who could barely make it across the school pool.

She jumped when Mum touched her shoulder.

"Melissa, Mrs. White would like to talk to you. She owns a gift shop in town. She's very interested in your float."

Melissa turned, her face lighting up. "It's so perfect," she said. "About *this* big. And like a rainbow."

"Will you sell it to me?" Mrs. White said abruptly.

"Huh?"

"I'll give you . . . ten dollars."

Melissa shook her head.

"You can buy a lot of candy with ten dollars."

"Candy's bad for your teeth."

"Books then. Whatever." The woman smiled. Melissa didn't like her smile. It wasn't quite real. She shook her head again.

"Twenty dollars. My last word. That's a lot of money for a young girl."

Melissa looked at Mum, but for once she was no help at all. "It's your find, love. Your decision." She walked away and left the two of them together.

"N-no," Melissa stammered. "Thank you."

The smiled became fixed. "Thirty dollars," the woman snapped. "Oh, come on now. If it's as good as you say I'll make it thirty-five. Think what you could do with thirty-five dollars!"

Melissa went on shaking her head dumbly.

"They're fragile things, these floats. You might not even get it home in one piece. Suppose you drop it? What have you got then? Nothing. Better take my offer."

Melissa was no longer listening. The boat had turned for shore, and she could hear the singing once again, high, sweet, piercing.

On the drive home Mum suddenly said, "That woman, what's-her-name, Mrs. White, said you were rude to her, Melissa."

"Was I?" said Melissa vaguely. "I didn't think I was."

As soon as Dad had parked she ran along the path. "Oh, hurry, where's the key?"

"My goodness, but you're jumpy." Mum unlocked the door with maddening slowness.

Melissa rushed into the living room. "It's still there."

"Of course it is, Silly Billy. Tell me, how much *did* that woman offer you for the float?"

"Thirty-five dollars." Melissa dropped into a chair and, elbows on the table, chin on hands, stared into the iridescent glass. She didn't notice the expression on her parents' faces.

"Thirty-five dollars!"

Dad whistled. "Which I suppose means she could sell it for twice that. That's an expensive bauble, Melissa. You'd better take care of it!"

They all stared at the float. Then . . . "I almost thought—but that's ridiculous." Mum shook her head as if to clear it. "Look, let's have a proper bake-out on the beach. That salmon we bought in Tofino. Will you get a fire started, Phil? I'll make a salad. Melissa, that thing's making me nervous. Will you please put it safely in your room?"

Melissa lifted the float from its bed of tissues and gasped.

"Hey, careful! You nearly dropped it then. Want me to look after it for you?"

"No, thanks, Dad. It's fine." Melissa walked quickly out of the room. The glass float was suddenly as hot as a baked potato. She put it safely down on her dressing table and rubbed her hands. The palms were pink and puffy. She stared at the float. Deep inside it something glittered and moved. She ran out of the room, her heart thumping, and went to help Mum dry the lettuce.

Sitting with her back against a log, Melissa licked the last of the salmon off her fingers and stared vaguely out to sea. The sun had set, and the dark was creeping up the beach with the incoming tide. Far out past their headland she could see the rhythmic flash-flash of a lighthouse. The wind rose and she shivered suddenly.

"Time to go in. Hot chocolate by the fire and then bed."

"Our last day tomorrow. I wish we could come back here for ever and ever."

"I second that." Dad kissed the top of her head. He began to pick up the remains of their meal, and Mum shook out the rug. Melissa followed them up to the cabin, suddenly reluctant to face whatever it was that moved within the float.

Mum lit the fire, and Dad stirred chocolate on the stove. Beyond the uncurtained window the blackness was broken only by the comforting lighthouse signal. Melissa drank her chocolate in very small sips. It was almost cold by the time she got to the bottom.

"Enough hanging around," Mum said at last. "Teeth and bed. Off you go." And she had to kiss them good night and go into her room.

She walked over to the dressing table and touched the float with a fingertip. It was as cool as . . . as cool as glass. In the semidarkness it was just a smoky glass globe, so fragile she could crush it just like *that*. She found she was holding it in the palm of her hand, her fingers closed tightly about it. She hadn't even re-membered deciding to pick it up. She put it down with a gasp, tore into her pajamas, and jumped into bed.

She fell asleep and into a muddled dream in which she was a princess, imprisoned by a magic spell in a tiny spherical house. Each day she grew weaker and weaker. One day she would be too weak to shine anymore and would cease to be. . . .

The singing woke her and she sat up, shivering, still in the sadness of her dream. From the dressing table came a faint rosy glow. She could see its reflection in the mirror. Surely she wouldn't have imagined *that*?

"What is it?" she whispered desperately. "What do you *want*?"

Freedom. The word slid into her mind, and it was the right word, the word behind the singing and the dream.

"How?"

You know how. In her mind was the picture of her hand holding the float, her fingers tight about it, crushing.

"Break it? I couldn't. Not possibly." She buried her head in the pillow and pulled the covers over her ears to muffle the sound of singing. Or was it weeping?

Next morning, after making her bed and dusting her shells—she didn't feel up to touching the float— Melissa had breakfast and ran down the beach until the sea seethed around her bare toes and the tide tugged at her ankles. Then she turned to look along the shore. The very last day. Where shall I go? What shall I find?

But the magic was quite gone. Suddenly it didn't

matter whether she walked south or north. It wasn't important to find another perfect shell. Nothing mattered.

In the end she walked south along the creamy edge of the sea, scuffing the wet sand with her toes, her hands in her pockets. She trudged all the way to the southern headland, which was covered with barnacles and mussels and great red and purple starfish. Then she turned and trudged slowly back.

All the colors seemed to have drained out of the sea and the sand. Melissa shivered and looked up at the sky. The sun was shining steadily, and there wasn't a cloud in sight. Then the singing began again, very faintly, as if whoever it was had moved farther away. Or was, perhaps, becoming weaker.

She sat on a log with her head in her hands. "What am I to do? Oh, I wish I'd sold it to that horrid woman. Then I'd have the thirty-five dollars and none of this worry." But she knew, as soon as she said it, that her wish wasn't true. Mrs. White wasn't the kind of person to pay attention to the singing, even if she could hear it. And she would *never* let the float go.

"Neither can I," thought Melissa desperately.

Then she heard Dad calling her and she had to run along the beach with a happy smile on her face and be very excited about a trip down the coast to Ucluelet.

They had a splendid dinner out, to celebrate the last night of the holidays, and for whole minutes at a time Melissa was able to forget. But eventually they drove up the dark winding road to the cabin, and Melissa had to open her bedroom door and go in.

There was no color at all in the globe tonight, and the singing was fainter than the sound of the sea. "If I just hang on," she told herself, "it'll stop altogether and then I'll just have a beautiful float."

No you won't, a small voice inside said coldly. It'll be a coffin. For something. For someone.

She sighed heavily, got into her pajamas, and brushed her teeth and kissed Mum and Dad good night. Then she sat up in bed with the pillow at her back and her arms tightly around her knees, waiting. She knew exactly what had to be done.

The quiet voices of Mum and Dad stopped at last. A long time later a silveriness at her window told Melissa that the moon must be high over the sea. She got out of bed and put on her slippers. Then she picked up the float and quietly opened the front door.

The path to the beach was striped with moonshine and shadow. She held the float in both hands until she was safely down on the sand. The tide had reached the high mark. There was no wind, and the water was almost still, with just a faint swell like the breathing of a giant. The silken path of the moon lay from the horizon almost to her feet.

It was the right time and the right place. She held the float with a tissue around it to protect her hand. Then she shut her eyes and squeezed.

It took much more pressure than she had expected.

I can't, she thought. I can't. Then, quite suddenly, it collapsed. She had a flash of intense happiness and opened her eyes in time to see something dart into the moon's white path.

For an instant she saw clearly a beautiful face, small and pale as carved ivory. The lips smiled and the dark eyes glowed with joy. "Wait!" Melissa called, and her voice was shockingly loud in the stillness of the turning of the tide. "Tell me who you are."

The figure paused on its upward flight, and the gossamer robes curved about it in a prism flash of rainbow colors. You are a princess, Melissa found herself thinking, imprisoned by a Japanese ogre. How many years ago? She imagined her bobbing helplessly across the ocean, singing her sad song, until the day when at last wind and tide brought her to this beach and drew Melissa to her.

I set her free. Melissa drew a deep breath and savored the happiness that tingled through her whole body, making her feel more alive than she had ever felt before, so that she could understand the voice of the sea and the breeze, and smell each separate scent of salt and iodine, seaweed and pine tree, moonlight and night.

Then a small cloud slid for a moment across the moon. At once the white path was gone and with it the fairy princess. Melissa was alone, shivering and sad, with her hands full of shards of rainbow-shot glass. She wrapped the pieces carefully in the tissue and walked slowly back to the cabin and put them in the wastebasket in her room. She got into bed and turned her back on the moonlit stripe that lay between the not-quite-shut curtains.

Melissa woke to the bustle of packing. Breakfast was cereal and rolls, so as to dirty no more dishes than necessary.

". . . and give me your glass float, Lissa, and I'll pack it among all our soiled clothes. It'll be as safe as houses there."

Melissa tried to swallow a piece of roll that had turned into a lump of concrete as all the misery of the night before came flooding back. "It's broken. I broke it."

"Oh, Lissa . . ." Mum began, then stopped. "Never mind, love. Bring me your other treasures, and I'll see they get home safely."

It began to rain as they started out. By the time they had reached the main road, the wipers were going full speed. Melissa sat in the back surrounded by bags and leaned her forehead against the seat in front. She tried to recapture that tiny moment of joy, but she couldn't. All that was left was this black heaviness.

I don't have my float, and I'll never find another. I don't even have the thirty-five dollars. I've got nothing.

She shut her eyes and tried to remember the rainbow colors that appeared and vanished as you turned the float in the light. Maybe she should have saved the pieces. Maybe in them would have been a tiny memory . . .

"Oh, look, Melissa!" Mum suddenly cried. "Did you ever see anything so beautiful!"

She looked up. The rain clouds had been torn apart and the sun had appeared in the gap. Directly ahead of them, arching from the headland to the sea, was a perfect double rainbow.

10
Uptown Local

by Diane Duane

Any wizard will tell you that there are two sorts of places where, without being put there on purpose, magic naturally comes to live. It favors the sort of empty places, far from the homes of men, on which people gaze with longing and wonder: lonely mountains, empty wastes of ice or fire, and of course that greatest, deepest emptiness, outer space. But magic also prefers the places where people have crowded together the most closely, for the longest time, to change one another and be changed themselves. On Earth right now, of the many such spots, three in particular are famous both here and in other worlds for their power and the lives they've changed. One is Westminster Abbey in London, where lie the Sword and the Stone, the tool and the seat of half a hundred kings and queens. Even in these modern days the power is undiminished, and the trampling tourists hush when they pass the plain round rock and the rusty blade. Another spot is the Capitoline Hill in Rome, where of old the Senate met to wield an empire's force over all the world they knew, and Romans from three continents gathered to hear them. But of the Three Great Places, more renowned than either of these is the New York City subway system.

This may sound odd at first, since the subway isn't one place, one spot, but a network. It will seem odd, too, because any adult and most kids you know who've ridden the subway will tell you instantly that it's dirty, run-down, and dangerous. And (much of the time) they'll be right. The danger lies in thinking that because the ugly part of this (or any other) story is true, the rest of it doesn't count.

Wizards try not to make this mistake. But even they have to work at it.

Nita and Kit were wizards. How they got that way has been told elsewhere, and isn't really so much of a big deal anyway, seeing that one out of every four people you meet is a wizard of some persuasion anyway. All you really need to know about Kit and Nita is that they could do magic, usually by reading it out of the wizards' manuals they'd found. They had been to the Moon and the bottom of the Atlantic (without using spaceships, submarines, or other artificial aids); had talked to trees and sharks and once to an Edsel;

had brought statues to life, saved the world, and walked on water. But since Nita was thirteen and Kit was twelve and both of them were at the height of their power and could do practically anything they set their minds to, they sometimes got incredibly bored. They were incredibly bored now.

"There's nothing on TV," Kit muttered, lying on Nita's living room floor and scowling at the *TV Guide*. "It's a desert."

"Yeah."

Nita was curled up on the couch, looking just as grim as Kit, and they both held their positions for several minutes.

Finally Kit pitched the *TV Guide* across the room. "Let's go bug Tom and Carl," he said, without much energy.

"Okay." Nita got up and they went outside together, walking down their suburban street because they were so bored that even teleporting seemed like too much trouble. Tom and Carl were the local Senior Wizards, whose business it was to advise the other wizards in the area; and as usual, if you didn't know they were wizards by being told, you would probably never know, because they both seemed perfectly normal. They shared a big house in a quiet part of town, and one of them worked for the big CBS station in the city, and the other one wrote stories and articles for his living. They had dogs, and a macaw, and a garden with too many snails in it (as Tom would repeatedly tell you when he was out picking them off the daisies), and cars that broke down sometimes, and everything else that people usually had.

Plus wizardry, which one out of four people have anyway.

Carl's Z80 was missing when they walked up the driveway; that was normal enough, since sometimes he had to go in to the station or to a business lunch on weekends. They rang the front doorbell. "It's open!" said a voice from inside.

In they went, through the very nifty living room with the wide-screen TV (Carl made a lot of money) and into the back room, where Tom's office was. Annie the sheepdog jumped up and licked their faces and got dirt all over them as they came in. Tom was at his computer: a tall, clean-cut-looking man hammering away furiously at the keyboard, while the screen in front of him filled up with green.

"Good to see you," Tom said, which was funny because he hadn't even turned around. "What can I do for you?"

"I think maybe we need an adventure," Kit said.

Tom sighed. "Can you come back later? I'm pushing a deadline."

"Tom, this is serious. We're gonna die if we don't find something to do."

"Try your backyards. If you can't find adventure there . . ."

"Tom!!"

"Don't push him. He'll stick us with doing a good deed," Kit said, looking grim. "Or something with a moral."

"What do you think this is?" Tom said, very patiently, not stopping his typing for a second. "Saturdaymorning TV? This is the *world*. It doesn't have a moral; it *is* a moral. The problem is figuring the story out. . . ."

"Oh my Loooooooord," Nita groaned. "Tom, give us a break, we're not in the mood."

"And as for good deeds," Tom said, making a mistake in his typing and backspacing frantically, "you're wizards, you couldn't *not* do them if you tried. You take Carl, now, he—"

"I can't believe this," Kit moaned. "We're going out of our minds and he's telling us stories! Tom, *do* something!!"

"I am doing something," Tom said. "I'm getting this ready for the Federal Express man, who will be here any second. After which time—"

"We'll never last."

"We will die right here on your rug."

"Probably stink the place up—"

"Right." Tom told the computer to save what he was doing, and turned to them. "The subway. You're going down the subway, both of you."

"Oh, come on!!"

"That's an adventure?"

"Don't read the papers, do you?" Tom *tsk*ed at them.

"But that's not the kind of adventure I mean. The place is the greatest reservoir of native wizardry on the East Coast, on this whole continent in fact. Enough to shut even you two up for a few hours. Take the subway."

They exchanged skeptical glances. "We've been to New York," Kit said. "And in this weather, the subway is the pits."

"You've been to *a* New York," Tom said. Nita and Kit looked at him oddly. He went rummaging through his top desk drawer, shut it, and, muttering, opened the next one down, a deeper one. "No, I'm not speaking figuratively. There's more than one universe, you know. The comic book writers have known it for years, and now the physicists are finally agreeing with them. Took them long enough. More than one universe, therefore more than one New York. You have subway fare?"

"Who needs to go through the turnstiles?" Nita said. "We can teleport in and just sink down through the sidewalk. Or walk through the walls."

"Shame on you," Tom said, sounding a touch severe. "You want the universe to die early? Huh? Then don't rip off energy. Wizards are for slowing down the energy running out of the universe, or for putting some extra back in—not for making everything run out of steam sooner. You use a system, pay for what you use. That's a dollar eighty."

Taken aback, Nita and Kit fished around for change, while Tom dug deeper in the drawer, turning over papers. Annie came over, looking interested, and put her head in the drawer. "No cookies for you," Tom said, rummaging. "Get out of here. Look at this mess," he said, resigned, coming up with a double handful of bizarrely assorted stuff and dropping it on the desk beside the computer.

"Wow," Nita said, taking the three quarters Kit handed her and then reaching out to take something hanging by a thin chain from the assortment of crumpled papers, dead batteries, credit card receipts, old check registers, and ballpoint pens run dry. On the chain was a shiny metal fish charm, the kind with a jointed body that moves a little when you bend it. "Like it?" Tom said.

"Yeah, it's neat."

"Take it. Carl got it out of a gumball machine. He gets so bored in the supermarket. . . . Besides, it's as good a key as any."

"Key?"

"Aha," Tom said, pouncing on something in the drawer. "Here." He held out his hand for the money. Nita passed him seven quarters and a nickel; Tom passed her two subway tokens. When she saw them she almost dropped them. In her hand they glowed as if they were red-hot, but they felt cold as ice.

"You can use these as many times as you need them," Tom said. "They have the transfer function built in. Just give them to someone else when you're ready to come home. Keys like that"—and he gestured at the little metal fish Nita held—"will influence where the trains take you. So will preferences that aren't physically embodied. Watch what you think while you're riding. And watch what you're carrying. Anything else you need?"

"Clearer instructions," Kit said, giving the fish a cockeyed look.

"Get on a train," Tom said. "Ride until you feel like getting off. Then have a look at where you've wound up. When you're tired of it, catch another train. *No* time traveling," he said, looking severely from one of them to the other. "You change history, you may not have a home left to come back to. Okay?"

"Okay."

"Which train should we take?"

"I am *not* going to tell you everything," Tom said with dignity, and turned back to his computer. Nita and Kit grinned at each other and headed out of the house.

"Speak to strangers," Tom said to their backs, pounding at the keyboard and not turning around.

They did teleport into the city—straight to Grand Central worldgate, the one hidden in the back of the cramped little deli by the Lexington Avenue Local entrance; and no one saw them (apparently) step straight out of the soda cooler, because almost no one in New York sees anything that doesn't speak to them first. Nita paused only long enough to buy a bag of Wise potato chips, her favorite, and then she and Kit headed out of the deli and around the corner, up the ramp that led toward the street doors and the Lexington Avenue Local entrance.

"Get your face out of the bag for a moment," Kit muttered, as they went down the steep stairs to the turnstiles. "Where're the tokens?"

"Here." She gave him one.

"Euuh! You got gunk on it!"

"You should talk? The Mud King of Nassau County?" Nita snickered at Kit's back as he went through the turnstile ahead of her, onto the crowded platform. She slipped her token into the machine and went after him. "After that last ride down Dead Man's Hill, I thought your mom was going to—uhh—"

She stopped dead, staring at her hand. The token was still in it. Or was in it again.

"Come on, kid, move it," said some weary New Yorkish voice behind her. Nita hurriedly slipped over to one side, where Kit was looking with as much surprise at his own hand. "It's back," he said. "And it's still got gunk."

"No pleasing some people," Nita said. She pocketed her token and headed down the platform.

There were a lot of people standing around; evidently the number six train was running late again. Nita picked a spot about halfway down the length of the platform, next to a young guy with a boom box, and spent a cheerful few minutes bopping to the music and ignoring the interested or disinterested looks of the people around her. Kit worked his way up the platform reading subway posters, and after a little while, at the rumbling sound of a train coming, came back to Nita and said, "That 'unicorn' is a goat."

"Huh? Oh, the Ringling Brothers one. Yeah, it's pitiful—" Anything else Nita would have said was lost in the scream and rumble of the train coming into the station. It was covered with graffiti; but as it slowed Nita began noticing something odd about it. The train stopped, and the doors opened, and Nita stood there for a second and let the other people brush past her. Someone had done the Mona Lisa on the side of the train. And there was a square of Marilyn Monroe heads, in Andy Warhol's style; and one of Dürer's floppy-eared rabbits; and the Dutch Masters. . . . The next car was completely covered (except for the windows) with a giant-size version of van Gogh's *Starry Night*.

Nita stared at Kit. Kit stared back. And all around them people shouldered their way into the train as if they saw nothing unusual at all.

"Fifty-first Street next; watch the closing doors," said the bored voice of the conductor over the loud-speaker, and Kit and Nita slipped into the train just as the doors were shutting. They grabbed a pole and hung on as the train did its traditional violent lurching start.

"Fifty-first?" Kit said, or rather shouted, over the rising clamor.

Nita shrugged and nodded.

The ride and the people on the train were perfectly normal: working people in jeans and T-shirts; joggers in warm-up suits heading uptown; some kids dressed very punk, one with blue and silver hair that Nita immediately began to envy; businessmen in suits and ties, with one hand reading papers folded the long way and with the other hanging onto straps, oblivious. "Fifty-first Street," said the conductor, and the train began to slow.

Nita swung around her pole and braced herself against the sides of the door as the train screeched and jerked to a stop. She stepped out cautiously and was almost trampled by a little troop of incoming businesswomen in jackets and skirts and jogging shoes. Kit pulled her aside, out of the way, and they looked around them at the little station. There were all the usual things one expects to see: cracked, stained wall tile; a floor well stained with blots of bubblegum; peeling paint on the rails of the stairs going up toward street level; a subway map much worn at the Fifty-first Street stop from being touched a million times; beside it, a poster of the Eyewitness News Team, all wearing mustaches, even the women. Behind Kit and Nita, the train pulled out, thundering. Its last car was decorated with a wraparound mural version of the ceiling of the Sistine Chapel.

"Come on," Kit said, and headed up the stairs and out the swinging gate beside the turnstiles. Together they headed up the next flight of stairs, which led to the street. Kit looked up at the darkish sky at the top of the stairs and said something vulgar in Spanish. "Great, it's gonna rain. . . ."

And he trailed off as Nita slipped ahead of him and put her hand out to something coming through the rails of the subway kiosk, from above ground level: flowers—a branch of dogwood, and on the other side some curling vines of cabbage rose. She glanced up and found that the darkness had nothing to do with rain. Trees hemmed the kiosk in. There was no sidewalk, no street . . . just the trees, immense and old, making their own twilight under a cloud-streaked sunset sky. That by itself would have been quite enough to astonish her; but then she noticed the clusters of tiny stucco houses clinging to various of the tree trunks like an architecturally minded fungus. And through the air, slipping among the trees as if among a stand of underwater weed, came swimming a placid school of smallmouth bass, silver-scaled except where the sunset struck through the trees and plated them with sliding gold.

Nita fingered Tom's toy fish on its chain, her "key," while behind her Kit goggled at the bass. Several of them goggled back briefly, making fish faces, and then swam on. *So it was true after all,* she thought. "You believe this?" she said aloud.

"*This* is New York??"

Nita looked across at the little houses and saw curtains being hastily pulled behind windows in several of them. "Not ours, that's for sure," she said. "Come on, let's try somewhere else. We're freaking the neighbors."

She turned and went back down the stairs. Cool iron-smelling air breathed up past them, and there was a faint rumbling down there, the sound and wind of another train pulling in. Nita felt in her pocket for the token, found it, put it in the turnstile, bumped through; then the token was in her hand again, and Kit came through behind her, holding a white rose in one hand, sucking a finger of the other where the rose had thorned him. The train roared in.

This one was old, one of the ancient thirties trains still pressed into service during peak periods, with enameled poles and straps made of real leather. It had graffiti on the outside too, of the usual spray-can sort, but the lettering was so strange that Nita wondered whether delinquent Martians had been sneaking over the barbed wire of the Bronx trainyards to "write" the trains. The cheerful bunch of Hispanic kids clustered by the front window of the head car, and all the other commuters inside, reading the *Post* or gazing out the windows, seemed not to notice, or care. . . .

"Fifty-ninth Street next," said the conductor over the ancient, staticky loudspeaker.

"Bloomingdale's?" Nita said.

"Why not?"

They got off, passed without comment a well-dressed

man banging fruitlessly at a jammed turnstile, and went up the stairs to the street. At least there *was* a street this time—the intersection of Lexington Avenue and Fifty-ninth—and Bloomingdale's was in its usual spot, but there all resemblance to the place where Nita's dad liked to shop abruptly ceased. The street in front of Bloomie's was filled with horse-drawn hansom cabs of all sizes and descriptions, and on the sidewalks strolled stylish ladies in long dresses with bustles, and men in what looked like tuxedoes. Evening was coming on: a lamplighter went by with the long pole used to light the gaslights in the street. But down Lexington Avenue a traffic light turned red, and across Fifty-ninth, several people were browsing in the window of an electronics shop, looking at videotape recorders and answering machines. . . .

"Look at that," Kit whispered. Nita looked up at the source of the ratchety sound that had attracted his attention. Dodging among the skyscrapers, in a blur of brass-and-glass dragonfly wings, came something like a helicopter . . . but noisier, less graceful, and far more ornate and bizarre. It darted between two tall office towers, heading for the broad upright of the Pan Am building, and sank out of sight.

"Ornithopter," Kit said. "Da Vinci did a design for one once. . . ."

Nita looked at Kit curiously. "What have you got in your pockets?"

"Huh? Oh—" He went through them, coming up

with a plastic key ring, some Dentyne, and some loose change, one piece of which was abnormally large.

"What's that?" said Nita.

"Oh, it's a shilling. English. My dad gave it to me; he was cleaning out his drawers . . ." Kit paused and looked toward Madison Avenue. A hotel had twin flagpoles sticking out from it, and a soft evening breeze slipped down the Avenue and rolled the flags out on the air. They were both the Union Jack.

"Huh," Nita said. "This New York is still a colony. . . ."

"C'mon," Kit said, and went back down the subway. "Let's see what else we can come up with."

"Watch what you think, Tom said."

"So watch me. I'm thinking."

Air rushed up around them again as they went down the stairs, but there was little sound. This was surprising, but only until the train—this one sleek, bare silver—came hurtling into the station without bothering to touch the track with anything, including wheels: it had none. It stopped with the silent abruptness of a vehicle using either artificial gravity or an inertialess drive as a motive force. It had no doors. What it did have were places where its walls suddenly stopped being: out of these came assorted business people, some school kids with book bags, and a mumbling bag lady.

"Sixty-eighth Street next," said the train in a dulcet voice like someone announcing the time over the phone, "watch the closing dilations."

They got in and for the first time in their lives had a subway ride that did not require hanging on to anything; except for stanchions and ancient lightbulbs flashing past, and the whoosh of wind, they might have been standing still. Then, flick! they *were* standing still, and the clean new tile of the Sixty-eighth Street station was spread out in front of them. Kit led the way up the stairs with a concentrating look on his face.

At first look around, on street level, Nita thought he had blown it. All she saw were the usual buildings and stores, the heart of Hunter College—and then she blinked. When had Hunter's buildings ever been surrounded by so many trees, a little forest of them?—and when had those buildings ever been such a mass of spires and stained glass and flying buttresses? Gargoyles grinned down everywhere; even the Seven-Eleven a little way down Lexington had become a lovely thing, all diamond-paned glass and half-timbered walls, and a roof that was actually thatched. In and out of ornate doorways people passed, dressed in rich clothes: furs and velvets, cloaks, sumptuous academic robes. Gems and gold glittered on passersby in the warm afternoon sunlight. And were those policemen, walking along and chatting calmly in knightly surcoats of night-blue velvet and silver, with long, bright swords hanging at their hips? Nita opened her mouth, looking up at the white towers of Hunter, and then shut it again, as wheeling overhead she saw the dragon go by, glittering, black winged and immense.

"Not bad, huh?" Kit said.

"What were you thinking of ?" Nita said, as over-head the dragon burst into song like a chorus of merry thunders.

"Dungeons and Dragons."

"Where are the dungeons?"

"Don't ask. C'mon, your turn."

She headed down the stairs, trying not to stare as they were followed downward by several people dressed like young kings, and a snow-white, one-horned beast that was definitely not a goat.

So the afternoon went, and as it went along, it began turning into a competition—the two of them vying to produce the brightest New York, the darkest one, the most extravagant, the emptiest. They changed sub-way lines several times, for more variety. On the dou-ble A line, Kit found a Central Park full of friendly dinosaurs, and got his foot stepped on by an over-affectionate Triceratops, so that he limped for a couple of days thereafter. Nita found a New York where single-minded robots trundled up and down steel streets, and a self-propelled garbage truck tried to remove her and Kit as refuse. Probably in reaction, Kit immedi-ately found a Manhattan entirely inhabited by talking beasts, some of whom could be seen walking humans on leashes; they did not spend much time there. Nita found a stop on the D train that gave onto a New York in the middle of an ice age, where polar bears stalked deserted streets in the screaming, snowy wind. Kit found a New York sunken like Atlantis, in water that they could breathe; fish were nesting in the drowned trees, and the Empire State Building was smothered in white coral, a blind-walled ghost of itself in the wet green-blue twilight.

How is it happening? Nita thought as she and Kit came up from a stop on the F train's line into a moonlit Manhattan completely devoid of buildings or streets, one huge park from river to river. *Are we finding these places? Or are we making them somehow?* The only answer was the high melodious, howl of a wolf from the northward, joined a second later by a second voice, and a third.

"Come on," she said, "watch this." Down the stairs she went again, back through the turnstiles, concentrating fiercely. A D train came thundering in. "What're you going for?" Kit hollered in her ear.

"Shush!"

The train came, the only odd thing about it being the presence of an actual locomotive puffing steam. They got on and rode in silence, accompanied only by a drunken gentleman talking peacefully to himself, and a pretty black girl in pegged pants and a Walkman, singing along inaudibly under the train's roar. Nita let several stops go by, thinking hard, losing her concentration, finding it again. *If we make them, then why not . . . why not . . .*

The train stopped and Nita jumped up, knowing this was the spot, whether she'd gotten it right or not. The doors opened, and she practically sprinted out of them, Kit coming close behind. Up the stairs she went and then stopped and stood panting at ground level, at Forty-second and Fifth, right by the library.

It was their own world. The green-painted news-stand was right by the kiosk where it should have been, behind them the library reared up white and solid, and across Forty-second was the usual row of stores. Traffic was running as usual. Nita breathed more slowly. *I did blow it*, she thought. . . .

"No horns," Kit said.

She glanced at him, then looked out in shock at the traffic. It was moving with quick efficiency, and no horns were blowing, and the drivers all looked alert but good-humored. Nita began to watch the pedes-trians, then, in growing wonder. It was apparently lunch hour, and they were striding about their busi-ness with the usual New Yorkers' energy; but the faces were merry, or eager, or cheerful, or interested, or thoughtfully calm—*all* of them. No look of boredom, or worry, or anger or pain or hunger, was to be seen anywhere. And the street was clean, and when the light changed there was no gridlock—

"The druggies are gone," Kit said. And sure enough, the guys who usually stood at this corner at lunch-time, saying (apparently to themselves), "Smoke, smoke, smoke . . . " were entirely missing. Nita, slowly smiling, could understand it. None of these busy, in-volved, glad people looked like they needed drugs. . . .

"But it's ours," Kit said. "Our world—"

"Real close," Nita said. "Kit—why couldn't *ours* be like this—"

"It would take forever. . . ."

"Would it? This took just a few minutes."

"We're wizards. . . ."

"So is twenty-five percent of everybody alive. Most of them just don't know it, that's all. Not five minutes, maybe, but a year, five, ten—"

"How?"

Nita let out a breath. "I don't know."

Kit looked at her and shook his head. "Let's walk a little," he said.

She sighed and went after him. This place seemed too good to be true, but it was true. *Why not, why not?!* The thought kept singing in her head as they crossed the street and she saw the sun glance fierce and bright off the Chrysler Building as off an upheld spear. There must be a way.

They stopped long enough to buy a hot dog apiece from a vendor and eat it where they stood. Then, "I'm getting tired," Kit said.

Nita wasn't even slightly tired, but she said, "Okay. Where now?"

"One more ride?"

"Sure. Where?"

"I want to go to Kennedy and see the planes, while we're so close."

It was likely to be three-quarters of an hour's ride,

but Nita shrugged. "Okay."

They went down to the D train station under Rocke-feller Center and caught a Train-to-the-Plane, one of those special trains that normally cost more. No one asked them for an extra fare, though, and they found a forward-facing window seat and settled in, for the plane train makes some of its run above ground, on elevated tracks that give a good view. The train made its usual underground stops in Manhattan, howled along through the tunnels below the river, and then burst out into bright Brooklyn sunlight and climbed above the brick and tarpaper rooftops, hooting merrily.

They stared out the window and watched the forest of chimneys and antennas and water tanks go by. Slowly the path of the train declined, curving southward, and passed Aqueduct Racetrack with its acres of parking lots. Sunset was approaching: the east was darkening blue.

Houses grew few, and the streets began to be lined with factories and warehouses, or with broad round tanks that said TEXACO or SHELL, full of kerosene for jets to burn. "It looks the same," Nita said to Kit. So it did: for after Aqueduct even the factories went away, and they turned a last broad curve lined on both sides with great empty stretches of reeds and cattails, hissing softly in the early evening wind. Then the train pulled in at the last stop, the Howard Beach stop that served the airport. They got out and walked up the usual creaking wooden walkway into the dingy little station building and out to the driveway circle where the buses waited that would take them across the miles of parking lots to the Kennedy terminals. Out the door and down the little ramp they went, and under the evening sky they paused, listening to the marsh and the sea birds crying, and the wind off Jamaica Bay—

. . . And the sudden thunder before them, and a light like a lance of fire, leaping upward, shaking the air in their lungs for as long as it remained in atmosphere—then, burning with impossible brilliance, turning every color of the rainbow in order, and flaring searing blue as it went into warp drive and vanished. Riding that tail of fire had been a graceful teardrop-shaped starship the size of a city block.

Nita looked at Kit in astonishment—and then at the front of the bus, which said KENNEDY SPACEPORT—SHUTTLE, TERMINALS A–F.

They got on the bus.

They rode once right around the terminal circle, just to see the docking cradles and the hangars, the great round or teardrop-shaped ships being pumped full of reaction mass from the Bay—for these ships were direct-mass converters that used the same fusion process the Sun did and could crack fuel-quality hydrogen out of any compound (such as water) that had some. They watched the catering trucks, and the little Port Authority flitters and ion-drive craft going about their business; they watched the hundreds of thousands of passengers, only some of them human, going in and out of the terminals with their luggage floating or walking behind them. And at the far end of the circle they got off the bus and went up onto the observation deck behind the space commuter terminal to look out across the field. There they gazed down along the eighteen-thousand-foot runway built into Jamaica Bay, and had the ultimate satisfaction of seeing the first of the space Shuttles, old *Enterprise*, drop like a graceful stone onto the runway, silhouetted against the burning sunset and the uprearing towers of Manhattan. Far above, the evening star was coming out, and the air smelled of kerosene and cooling tarmac. Nita sighed. *Enterprise* rolled to a stop, and the support trucks rolled up with the stairs, and commuters from the L-5 stations in orbit started coming out, jostling one another with their briefcases.

"Nostalgia," said a voice from beside them. "No one cares about those old workhorses anymore. It's the starships, the big cruisers, that everyone finds romantic."

Nita and Kit looked over to one side. There was a man leaning on the railing: quite old, and balding on top, but with an erectness about his posture that made them wonder why he needed the cane that was leaning on the Plexiglas beside him. He was well dressed in a sort of a cross between a jumpsuit and a business suit; and if his eyes were deep and old, they were also fierce. He looked a little dangerous.

Nita had heard so many people talking to themselves

that day that she almost didn't react. But there was a sad sanity about the man that tugged at her somehow, and suddenly Tom's memory spoke inside her, saying *Speak to strangers.*

"Why don't they care?" she said. "About the Shuttles, I mean."

The man looked at her in surprise, then settled on the railing again, watching the great rolling tender come out to lean the Shuttle back upright and attach its booster tanks. "Earth orbit," he said, "what's that? Who cares about the Moon? Space is open to a hundred light-years out now . . . but the outward move's stopping there. The government isn't interested in any more exploration. They want money now, and safety. Leave the exploring to other worlds, they say. We're comfortable. Why stick our necks out?" His voice was full of scorn. "And the mercantiles agree with them. Everything I've done has come down to making bankers fat. The heart, the joy, they're gone. . . ."

"I've never been on the Shuttle," Nita said. The man looked at her strangely.

"It's that way where we are too," Kit said, and for the second his voice was as fierce as the man's eyes. "They don't believe in going to space just to go anymore. They go because they're scared someone else will do it first, or because someone might make some money."

"The stars," Nita said, sorrowfully. "I'd give a lot just for a base on the Moon."

The man looked at them more strangely than before, taking in their clothes, the look of them. "Where are you from?" he said slowly.

"New York," Nita said.

"Not this one," said Kit.

"Not this—" The man broke off. "Do you know who I am?" he said.

They looked at him and shook their heads.

In the east, over the Bay, the Moon was coming up just past its full. The man turned to gaze at it with an odd, angry love. "And—where you come from—there's no Jura Base, no Tycho Dome? No Tranquillity Center?"

"No," Nita said.

"Not yet," said Kit.

"But there is a space program—"

"Just the Shuttles. They talk about a space station and the Space Telescope, but not much more." Kit shuddered. "A few planetary probes. There are lots of satellites, though. Some that kill each other with lasers."

The man took his cane away from the Plexiglas and leaned on it, and still stood straighter than anyone Nita could remember. "Show me," he said.

She began to shake. "You might not be able to get back."

"I don't care," the man said.

And it was plain he didn't. So they showed him. They slipped out of the commuter terminal a side way—

the man said there were people he wanted to avoid—
and caught the shuttle bus for the Howard Beach station. Nita went through the turnstiles first, pitching
her token over for their guest to use. Under blue evening they made their way back to Manhattan on a train
completely graffiti'd over, inside and out, but for a few
neglected windows. The man looked at all this in astonishment. But that was nothing compared to his
amazement when they hit their first Manhattan station
and he saw the oldness of it, the grime, the bitter or
wild or lively faces that waited for the train. And the
ads, the posters on the walls, fascinated him. "Tele-
vision," he said, as if it were an alien word. "Auto-
mobiles. It could be the dawn of the Age."

Nita's thought, though, was that it was getting too
dark for her and Kit not to leave: Both their parents
would pitch a fit. "We have to go home," she said.

"I *am* home, I think," the man said.

Kit looked at him hard, wanting to be sure he understood. "It's *not* where we found you."

"It's home," the man said, fierce eyed. And then he
looked out the window like a child seeing wonders. "It
could be different," he said. "This time."

The train was stopping near Port Authority. Nita
and Kit got up. Nita held out her token to the man.
So did Kit. "In case you need to get back," Kit said.

The man took them, his eyes shining.

" 'Bye," they said.

"The same to you," said the man.